AF663076

ON THE ROAD TO TARASCON

ARNAB NANDY

olive turtle

NIYOGI BOOKS

Published by
NIYOGI BOOKS
Block D, Building No. 77,
Okhla Industrial Area, Phase-I,
New Delhi-110 020, INDIA
Tel: 91-11-26816301, 26818960
Email: niyogibooks@gmail.com
Website: www.niyogibooksindia.com

Editor: Saachi Khurana
Design: Nabanita Das

ISBN: 978-93-86906-15-1
Publication: 2018

Printed at: Niyogi Offset Pvt. Ltd., New Delhi, India

For Dida.

FACT

The Painter on the Road to Tarascon (1888) is assumed to have been destroyed in a fire inside the Stassfurt salt mines in April 1945. Two fires took place at the mines—where the painting was stored along with more than 400 others of the Kaiser-Friedrich Museum—on 12 and 30 April, record declassified US military documents.

There is no clear evidence of how the fires caught—whether by accident or design. Dr Tobias von Elsner of the Kulturhistorisches Museum (former Kaiser-Friedrich Museum), Magdeburg, believes they were likely to have been arson, and started as a diversion to loot the priceless artworks. The Vincent van Gogh painting was the most important one in the museum's collection and this made it particularly attractive to looters. But who the looters were is difficult to say. They could have been American soldiers, Nazi officials, German civilians or forced labourers.

Evidences that have surfaced over the years indicate that some of the paintings may have survived. According to a report in the September 2009 edition of *The Art Newspaper*, a manuscript by Martin Luther, which had been stored at the

Stassfurt mines, was handed over by an American soldier to a military chaplain in 1945. This was later deposited at the Concordia Historical Institute in St. Louis, Missouri, US. It was returned to Magdeburg in 1996. An 1829 painting by the German artist Carl Hasenpflug—recorded to have been stored in the mines (though, the report says, it is not impossible that the painting had actually been stored in the vaults of the central bank in Magdeburg)—surfaced in 1950. Some partially burnt documents and artefacts were also recovered from the mines.

The Stassfurt mines stopped production in 1972 and were sealed. It is now impossible to enter the place where the paintings had been stored.

The Kulturhistorisches Museum authorities have been appealing to people who might have any information regarding the whereabouts of *The Painter on the Road to Tarascon* to come forward.

PROLOGUE

The artist walked backwards until his back touched the wall of his small studio at Arles in southern France. He scratched his beard and then chewed the end of a painting brush as he looked critically at the canvas that was bathed in afternoon sunlight.

The room had a big window facing south-west. A long narrow table—almost the entire length of the wall—stood right next to the window; on it lay strewn colours and brushes of various shapes and sizes. On the right end of the table stood a half-empty jug of water along with an empty glass. The 49x45-cm canvas stood at an angle a foot from the left end of the table. In front of it sat a wooden stool that the master used when he got tired of standing for hours.

'*Dit zou beter zijn geweest*,' he mumbled. *This could have been better.*

He decided the painting wasn't good enough to merit his signature. He chucked the paintbrush on the table and turned towards the door. He was hungry.

The sunlit canvas depicted a happy Mediterranean summer day.

The man wore a straw hat, an old grey full-sleeved shirt with dark blue trousers. He had a bag attached to his back—painting equipment. In his right hand was a reddish-brown bag with more painting equipment peeping out of it. He held a thin brown walking stick in his left hand and had a folded canvas tucked under the same arm.

The bright, not-yet-midday sun cast a dark shadow beneath him on the street, made remarkable by the master's clever patterns—mostly in yellow, golden and brown. Behind the figure stood two trees by the edge of the road. The one on the right had significantly more leaves. Beyond the trees lay agricultural fields—huge swathes of bright yellow and green—and beyond the fields some more trees, a couple of houses and the hint of a few hills.

The sky was blue with a single patch of white cloud peeping from behind the leafy tree on the right.

'To Herr Alfred Flechtheim,' the curator of the Kaiser-Friedrich Museum said as he raised the glass of wine, 'for giving us the opportunity to display this masterpiece.'

All eyes in the little group that had come to the painting's inauguration turned to the art dealer, as he nodded in acknowledgement and pointed to the 49x45-cm painting, which now occupied the pride of place in the museum's Fine Arts Gallery.

From the time it acquired the painting in 1912, the Kaiser-Friedrich Museum displayed the work continuously in its Fine Arts Gallery, even through the First World War.

Then the Second World War broke out.

1943

BLACK CLOUDS LOOMING

The tall thin man in his early forties trudged into his office, closed the door, went around the desk and sat on his chair. From his face, it was impossible to guess what was going on in his mind.

He placed his elbows on the desk and held his head in his hands. After a few minutes of sitting in silence, he clenched his jaw and forcefully brought down both fists on the desk together.

His secretary knocked and peeped in. 'Herr Bormann, is everything okay?'

'Yes, thank you. I'm just a little disturbed,' he said in an emotionless voice.

'Do you need anything?'

'No thanks. Just leave me alone for a while, please.'

'Of course, sir,' said the secretary and closed the door.

The curator's officer at the Kaiser-Friedrich Museum in Magdeburg was basic, with a desk at the end of the room, opposite the door. Four chairs stood in front of the long desk that had papers stacked on it.

The man sat back in his chair and looked out of the window on his left. This was a job he loved doing. It was more than a job; it was a passion. But things had not been going well for Jonas Bormann since he took charge as curator of the museum 10 months ago.

Today, the decision had been taken to move the paintings, and he did not like it one bit.

'And it's all because of that madman called Hitler,' he screamed inside his head, even though his face remained perfectly calm. Outside your home, revealing emotions was dangerous at a time when Nazi spies were practically everywhere.

In his mind, Herr Bormann started listing everyone and everything he hated. The war, of course. He was sick and tired of it. But the war wouldn't have started in the first place had it not been for Hitler. Then there were the Brits, because it was the fear of British bombings that had forced them to take the decision of moving the paintings.

The curator realised that at that point he hated pretty much everything other than his wife Claudia and the paintings under his care at the museum.

Of course, Herr Bormann understood the museum's art collection was being moved with the best intentions in mind. However, though he agreed this exercise could probably save them from British bombings, it certainly would not work too well against thieves and plunderers, especially if the enemy managed to reach Magdeburg.

Despite Herr Bormann's misgivings, the plan seemed to make the most sense at that point of time and he had not been able to come up with a better alternative, anyway. It had been decided that they would be sent to some abandoned salt mine. Apart from protection against bombings, the water-absorbing quality of the salt in the mine would also save the paintings from the moisture in the air.

On an overcast afternoon, 402 paintings from the museum were carefully packed by trusted workers under the watchful eyes of Herr Bormann and loaded onto two trucks. They worked as silently and as discreetly as they could. By the time they finished, it was close to 10 pm. The loaded trucks, along with the curator and the workers, remained at the museum for the night.

At first light the next morning, the curator, two other museum officials, and the workers left with the trucks for Stassfurt, a town situated 30 kilometres away from Magdeburg. It was windy, and the sky looked ominous, the curator thought, as the first rays of the sun made their way through the thick clouds. A frown never left his forehead as he worried about the paintings, especially #395. That was the closest to his heart and if he had to, if things came to that, he would probably trade all the other 401 works for that one painting—certainly not a line of thinking the museum authorities would appreciate, but that was just what he thought.

At the mine, Herr Bormann watched as all the paintings of the museum were stored 460 metres below sea level in huge chambers that remained after the salt had been removed. He ensured that each painting was packed and stored as safely as possible.

Before leaving, he whispered to painting #395, 'Stay safe, my friend.'

Though Herr Bormann was not aware of it at that moment, a top-secret factory making jet engines for the Germans operated just 30 metres above the chambers where the paintings were stored. At Stassfurt, the Germans also kept their largest stock of uranium, which the Allies feared the Nazis would use to build an atomic bomb. Consequently, it was no surprise that, when the Americans eventually reached Stassfurt in 1945, their immediate priority was to take possession of the salt mine and its surrounding areas.

Herr Bormann did not sleep well that night, and on several nights afterwards. There was not a waking moment when he was not trying to come up with a feasible plan to protect that one painting. Yes, it would of course hurt if the other works of art were damaged or destroyed. But if anything happened to that one, it would absolutely break his heart. Even when some ideas came to him, he certainly did not have the resources to carry them out.

What he really needed at that point was a resourceful friend.

Eight hundred kilometres away, another man tossed and turned in his bed. Richard George Pemberton, too, was thinking about the same painting.

2011

THE LAST MEETING

The young woman jumped out of the tram and walked with brisk steps. It was 11.03 am and she was supposed to be at her destination at 11 am. When she reached the seniors' home three minutes later, the woman at the lobby asked her to wait.

She sat playing with her thumbs and index fingers. It was an old habit that her friends often teased her about. But she had come here alone. She stopped when she caught another woman, who was sitting a few chairs away and looked roughly the same age as herself, staring at her fingers.

Five minutes later, when she laid her eyes on her grandmother after nearly two years, she had the feeling that this was going to be their last meeting. Claudia was 91 years old. A caregiver moved her around on a wheelchair and her speech was often incoherent. Her first-floor room at the seniors' home, situated on the outer fringes of the city, was comfortable and airy. It had big windows that overlooked a park. The visitor could see a number of old people walking to and fro in it. Several were moving around on wheelchairs. The area had been built as a refuge for the elderly with everything they could need situated close by. The caregiver had shown the woman into Claudia's room and left.

Her grandmother was sitting on a couch by the bed, looking through the window. She was small and looked almost shrunken, thought the visitor. She was in light blue pyjamas and her hair had been cut short. Her glasses lay on the bed.

The woman walked ahead and gently rested her hands on her right shoulder. 'How are you, Grandma?'

'Who is it?' Claudia turned around slowly and spoke in a German drawl.

'It's me, your granddaughter.' She smiled. It was true she had not spent enough time with Claudia, but they did have some happy memories. She picked up the pair of glasses from the bed, put them on the old woman and knelt before her.

'Oh,' she said, peering at her. 'It's been a long time, dear.' Claudia's eyes brightened for a moment, but just as quickly the flicker died. She seemed to have forgotten that she was meeting her granddaughter after ages. Almost mechanically, she turned her gaze again towards the window and continued to look at whatever she was looking at.

'How are you?' she asked again.

'I am bored,' Claudia said after a moment's silence, and sighed deeply.

'But now I am here, Grandma!' the granddaughter tried to enliven the moment.

Claudia kept gazing through the window. She was unable to remain focused on a single thing, the doctor had said.

'What are you bored of, Grandma?' she asked.

Claudia turned to her. 'Life.'

'But you have had such an interesting life. And I am sure you still have a ways to go.' She did not really feel in her heart what she had just said. Her gut said Claudia would be gone in the next few weeks.

'*Interessant, aber traurig*,' Claudia said in her soft cracked voice and pointed to a cardboard box by her bed. *Interesting, but sad.*

'Do you want me to bring it?'

Claudia nodded.

The box was quite light. The woman brought it and placed it between the two of them. 'Do you want me to open it, Grandma?'

Claudia nodded again.

It was full of knick-knacks—an old book, a fountain pen, several pictures...She picked up a black-and-white picture of a woman in her twenties. 'That is you, isn't it?'

Once more, Claudia nodded.

'You look so beautiful! Who's this letter from?' She picked up a yellowed open envelope that just had 'Claudia' written on it. 'May I?'

She nodded again.

She carefully pulled out the old sheet of paper from the envelope. It was nearly falling apart. Her eyes first went to the signature at the bottom. She read aloud: '"Edward Bates; Calcutta; 15 June 1945." That's a really old letter! Who is Edward Bates?'

Claudia knitted her brows in an effort to remember. Then she said in a matter-of-fact way, 'My lover.'

The woman couldn't stop herself from giggling. 'Are you serious?'

Claudia smiled for the first time that day. Innumerable lines spread across her face like cracking earth.

'But Grandma, this is in English. You can't read English, can you?'

She kept quiet for a while and then said, 'Jonas had taught me well.'

'Tell me more. I am curious!'

'I cheated on Jonas with his friend. They were trying to save the painting together.' Claudia's dispassionate way of saying it surprised the woman a little. But then she reasoned that perhaps at 91, it didn't make much sense to make a big deal of stuff that happened decades ago and when the other people involved were probably dead. But the last bit interested her more than the extramarital affair itself.

'Save the painting? What painting?'

'A priceless one,' Claudia said in a barely audible whisper, as if no one else was supposed to hear this bit of information.

'Aha...' She was a little incredulous. She couldn't be sure if the old woman was imagining it all.

Claudia continued, 'He used to come to visit me when Jonas would be away at the gallery. Both of them died so early...'

'And the painting?'

'What painting?' Claudia had forgotten already.

'The priceless painting they had teamed up to save—that is what we were talking about,' she reminded her.

'Oh...It got lost.' Claudia heaved another deep sigh and turned towards the window again.

The young woman turned her gaze in the same direction as her grandmother's. The summer morning was bright and she could hear birds chirping. Two old men were walking their dogs—a Golden Retriever and a cream-coloured Labrador. A red car rolled in and parked outside the department store beyond the garden.

'You mean they could not save it?'

'No one knows,' Claudia said and stopped talking.

The young woman glanced through the letter and though it appeared no more than a lover's note, something struck her as odd, though she couldn't put her finger on it. But this only intrigued her more.

There was a gentle knock on the open door and she looked up. It was the caregiver.

'It's time,' the caregiver said with a smile and left.

Tens of questions were beginning to form in the granddaughter's mind at this point, but she did not know where to start, or how much she could rely on her grandmother's replies, most of which, she decided, could easily be the old woman's imagination. But then, old people, much like children, could at times be surprisingly sharp. So, she couldn't discount the possibility that she might have been talking sense about the painting. 'Grandma, would you mind if I kept this letter?'

The old woman did not speak. She appeared to be in a different world.

The woman slipped the letter in her bag and looked back at her grandmother. She suddenly felt a lump in her throat. Claudia had been such a lively character not too many years ago, and thoughts of mortality crowded the young woman's mind. She wished she had spent some more time with her grandmother.

She stood up and wiped a tear with the back of her hand. Then she bent down, kissed Claudia on the forehead, and left.

That was indeed the last time they met.

1944

THE INANE REQUEST

Richard arrived at the prime minister's Chartwell home a couple of months after the successful landing of the Allied troops in Normandy. Clemmie Churchill opened the door herself and directed him to her husband's study, where the man was dictating one letter after another to his secretary.

'How are you, my boy?' said the man from behind a cloud of grey cigar smoke as he gestured him to a large comfortable chair.

'I am fine, Uncle Winnie. Congratulations on the successful landing in Normandy!'

'Thank you, Richard. But the men on the ground are the ones who deserve to be thanked,' he said. 'Give me 10 minutes.'

'Of course, sir,' he said and smiled to himself. He could never get over the way Winston Churchill pronounced 's' as 'sh' because of a speech impairment.

Once he was done, after not 10, but 30 minutes, the man turned to Richard. 'Now tell me, what brings you to Chartwell?'

Richard looked at the secretary.

The prime minister took the cue and said, 'Could you give us a minute, Emily?'

'Of course, sir,' said the secretary and left the room, closing the door.

Richard brought his voice down a few notches. 'Uncle Winnie, I need your help. I know the war is on and this is no time to spend resources on other things. But I came to you because I know you are interested in art yourself, and you are the one person who could possibly care.'

Churchill blew another cloud of smoke but kept his eyes focused on the young man. 'Go on.'

Richard said: 'We are bombing Magdeburg left and right. As far as I know, the Kaiser-Friedrich Museum's paintings are now stored in an abandoned salt mine not far from the city. But even if the Allies occupy the salt mine and get access to the paintings, you cannot protect them from arson and thieves in general. Now that the troops have landed in Normandy and are pushing in, I believe the painting is in grave danger. If you could only see it, sir…I know no painter who can make use of the paintbrush the way this man did. The strokes and patterns…'

'Hmm,' the prime minister said with an expressionless face while continuing to puff on his cigar.

'We need to work fast if we want to save it. Right now, few people have the time and energy to care about art. Everyone is just trying to survive the war. But sir, these are the very things that separate us from animals. Being human is not just about living to see another day,' said Richard passionately.

Churchill smiled, looked at the ceiling, and then looked back to the young man. Then, he said, 'You know, Richard, you could make a good politician. You speak well and rather convincingly.'

'Er, thank you, sir. That is indeed a big compliment coming from you,' he said sheepishly, knowing fully well that Uncle Winnie was just being kind to the son of his childhood friend.

The prime minister continued, 'What you say is not incorrect, but let me also remind you of a few truths. The first of them is that this war has reduced many people to being no better than animals, sometimes worse. Have you heard the rumours of people turning into cannibals?'

'Yes, sir, I have.'

'Do you believe such things are actually happening?'

'I am not really sure what to believe, sir,' Richard said.

'The rumours are true, Richard. There have been instances of people indulging in cannibalism to survive. You talk about art and how it differentiates us from animals, but you should know that the most basic instinct of all living beings—humans and animals—is to stay alive, and that is what most people out there are trying to do,' said the man.

'You are right, sir.' Richard lowered his gaze. His pulse had crossed 100 a long time ago. This was a meeting he had planned and practised at home for weeks and now he was almost sure it wasn't going to turn out the way he wanted it to. Why couldn't this damn old powerful man just say yes to his proposition? Despite all the chaotic thoughts inside his head, all he could do was say quietly, 'This is not the right time for me to be making such an inane request.'

'...But that certainly does not mean I don't see a point in what you are saying,' continued Churchill.

Richard looked up. There was still hope.

'Richard, I have seen some works of this artist and I quite like him, too. The war could be over in the next six or seven months. We are getting closer and closer to Berlin every day and if you think it is such an incredible work of art, we will not have it wait out the war. We will get to work immediately and make every effort to save it.

'However, you must understand that I cannot possibly order the men to look out for a single painting in the time of war. I do have to answer to the public for my actions, after all, and if this were to go public in some way, I will have a lot of explaining to do, and I have neither the time nor the energy for all that. So, we need to work covertly. I will give you a couple of men to work with on this. If you need help with things, call up Emily. And Richard, let me tell you again, I cannot stress enough the importance of this information remaining with only the people concerned. Please remember that.'

'Of course, Uncle Winnie. It will stay that way. I cannot thank you enough for this.' At this point, Richard was practically dancing in joy inside.

'However, you will need to bear the cost of the mission. Can you do that?' the prime minister asked and looked at him with an eyebrow raised.

'Yes sir, I can.'

'What do you think we could do with it after the war?'

'Let's get hold of it first. We can sit and decide on that once the war ends. We could possibly give it back to the Magdeburg gallery.'

'Very well, then. Someone will get in touch with you on this by tomorrow. Goodbye now, Richard. I have a hundred things to do. And please send Emily in on your way out.'

Richard left Chartwell smiling. A crucial part of his plan had worked out just the way he would have liked it. One thing was for sure: if he ever got his hands on that painting, it was certainly never going back to Magdeburg.

2011–12

TWO GERMAN GIRLS

Kolkata is a happy place to be in December. It's already around two months since Durga Puja and the Bengalis have gotten over the sad fact that they have to wait another whole year for the grandest festival of the region. The weather is pleasant with cool sunny days and bright blue skies.

The elderly Bengalis and the little ones (whose style statements directly reflect those of their mothers) love nothing better at this time than donning their signature winter accessory—the monkey cap.

During Christmas time, hundreds of people travel hours from the suburbs to do nothing but walk the stretch of the decked-out Park Street, which ends up as crowded as the Mahakumbh Mela if you compare them on a per-square-metre basis. Around this time, Bengalis love to stuff themselves with cakes, pies, pastries, turkeys and anything else they think is associated with Christmas. It is also a great time for those who love to party, because tens of parties and events are organised every day at different places across the city.

I had started that December Sunday particularly early. The alarm went off at 4 am and I dragged myself out of bed. I love food walks but not when they take place at 5.30 in the morning. But then, you just don't say you're not interested if it's your girlfriend who'd sprung that idea while bubbling with enthusiasm.

I put the phone on speaker and dialled Tina's number as I brushed my teeth. Twenty minutes later, when I was done with brushing, pooping and showering, she had still not picked up. And to think it was her bright idea to go and have a Chinese breakfast at Tiretti Bazaar.

Annoyed, I drove to her Salt Lake shared flat and called her again. No response. I finally woke the gatekeeper of the apartment complex, who thankfully didn't abuse me too much for coming at this hour (I suspect he remembered the fat puja tip I'd given him not too long ago), and went in.

Tina's flatmate, Amrita, opened the door yawning. 'Damn you, Neil! Why don't you stay over here or have Tina over at your place when you guys are planning to leave early together? Why do you have to wake me up?' she said.

'I'm super sorry. I'll remember that next time,' I mumbled.

'Please do that,' she said as she walked back into her room and banged the door shut.

'Calm down,' I told myself as my mind conjured up 10 mean things to tell Tina when she finally woke up. I opened her door and went in.

After a tiny fight, the two of us—neither looking at the other—left for Tiretti Bazaar close to 6 am. I had to say the food walk was worth it and that it considerably lifted both of our spirits. After stuffing ourselves with fish-ball soup, pork buns, pork rolls and dumplings, we bought some sausages to cook at home. Then we drove back to Tina's place and slept till midday.

'Why do you get mad at me because I can't get up early?' said Tina after we'd woken up.

'Well, it was your idea in the first place and I'd expected you to be more excited about it,' I said.

'Sawweeee,' she baby talked. I'd never found that cute. 'Won't happen next time.'

We passed the afternoon lazing in the house and watching TV. Later in the evening, Tina, who worked at an advertising agency in Salt Lake, had some work to finish before office the next day, and I left. I reached my South Kolkata home around 9 pm and decided to retire early.

My phone beeped as I was getting into bed an hour later. Someone had messaged me on the hospitality exchange network called Couchsurfing, which is mostly used by travellers.

Guten Tag!

Hello!

Salut!

We are two girls, Hannah and me (Eva), from Germany, looking for good company in Kolkata at the beginning of next year for three days.

It would be great meeting up with you and enjoying the time at your place for three nights. We'd appreciate if you have some tips for us on what to do and see. And if you have the time, we could go out together as well and have a drink and eat at one of the local places.

We don't expect much; just some guidance would be nice.

I'm not sure how to describe us, but I'll try: Fun-loving, talkative, curious, spontaneous, friendly and shiny!

If there is anything you would like to know about us, don't hesitate to ask!

Looking forward to hearing from you.

All the best.
Hannah and Eva

I had started using Couchsurfing back in 2008 and had found it an amazing resource while travelling. It enables you to stay with local people in a new place you are visiting.

I replied with a 'yes' without thinking too much about it.

Actually, I did think. A lot. I had a number of things to consider. It's not that I hadn't hosted girls before, but Tina had asked me to stop the 'Couchsurfing thing' since the incident last July.

I had been hosting a Brazilian couple and a French girl for a few days. With all the heat and humidity, July isn't the best time to visit Kolkata. Plus, my studio apartment did not have air conditioning. On the last night, the four of us were drinking endless bottles of beer. After a while, the couple started kissing and it didn't stop there. I enjoyed the view for a while and turned towards the French girl to see her diving for my face. I didn't stop her.

I'd always thought Tina and I were friends first and a couple later. We had decided to have an open relationship.

And we'd talked about how, if either of us had a sexual encounter, we wouldn't have issues sharing it with the other. We often talked about other couples who were cheating on each other and how we were different and more mature.

But this was the first time such a thing actually happened for either of us. I told her. She went all quiet.

The next day, she told me to stop the 'Couchsurfing thing'. Apparently, all that maturity crap only worked in theory.

I had not accepted any Couchsurfing requests since then. But this time, I went on to Eva's profile and checked her out. Most of the people who had hosted her before described her as 'friendly' and 'fun'. I wouldn't say it was an extraordinary profile, but something about it gave me a good vibe.

I did not say anything to Tina about this and on a January afternoon, I picked up Eva and Hannah from the railway station.

The train from Delhi was nearly a day late and the girls looked really tired. I felt a little ashamed and started to wonder if I should apologise to them on behalf of Indian Railways.

Eva was around 5'7" and had unkempt short blonde hair. She wore a grey jumper and golden-rimmed spectacles, the kind I usually associated with middle-aged uncles. I am not really sure why, but I thought she had this Meg Ryan air about her. Hannah, on the other hand, walked with slow and measured steps. She was a couple of inches shorter than Eva and looked like someone who knew her way around India. Her brown jacket matched the colour of her hair.

We scrambled into my little blue hatchback and I wove my way through the afternoon traffic to my pad.

On the way, I learnt that Hannah was teaching German in Delhi University as part of an exchange programme and was staying in India for three months. This was her second visit to India and she had already travelled to Rajasthan, Mumbai and several places in South India.

Over the next two days, we went all over Kolkata—Sudder Street, The botanical gardens, College Street, the works. We took all sorts of public transport. The girls were particularly fascinated by the ancient trams and took lots of pictures. Hannah was impressed by Calcutta University and started seriously considering doing a Hindi course there (I have no clue why). She even spoke to the professors at the department and left her email with a professor who said he would get back with the details. Then we had paan from a popular shop in the locality called Kalpataru.

'I think it tastes like soap,' said Eva.

Evidently, paan is an acquired taste.

Two of the three nights they were in town, we had rum and coke after dinner. Eva was suitably impressed by Old Monk and the three of us would have a lot of interesting drunken conversations.

Eva was studying to be a journalist back home. While Hannah had a boyfriend, Eva was single.

Three quick drinks had made me more outspoken than I normally was. 'I think you're cute,' I told Eva as I poured in my fourth drink.

'*Danke.*' Eva smiled. 'I mean, thank you.'

'Are you going to make out now?' laughed Hannah.

'*Sei* still, Hannah!' Eva chided her.

I was enjoying the whole thing when it struck me. What the hell was I doing? I had a girlfriend who was not as open-minded as I'd thought she was. Yet, I just couldn't stop myself from getting attracted to this dimpled girl in uncle-glasses.

'Do you have a girlfriend?' Eva asked.

'Yeah.'

'Oh.'

An awkward silence followed. We went to bed soon after because the girls had to catch a morning flight back to Delhi the next day.

1945

A RESOURCEFUL FRIEND

Edward Bates reached Magdeburg on the morning of 9 January.

To say the journey from London to Magdeburg had been difficult and tiring was an understatement. He had entered the mainland through southern France and made the journey to the Swiss border mostly on foot. It took him almost two weeks. An RAF fighter had dropped a bomb around a hundred metres from the house where he was spending his last night in France. His trip through Switzerland was rather incident-free and he looked forward to the time when his country wouldn't be involved in a war. For anyone else, the riskiest part of the trip would have been getting into Hitler's Germany. Fortunately for him, an old contact was now the commanding officer at the border right there. He had let Bates in into the country without much trouble.

The hardest part was getting to Magdeburg. He spoke to as few people as he could and moved as discreetly as possible. He was almost caught by the Stasi on at least two occasions. One time, an officer had actually arrested him. Luckily for Bates, that officer didn't have any backup at that point and he could overpower him and break his neck without much difficulty.

Yes, Bates considered himself lucky to be alive. But considering the time and place in history he was living in, that was by no means a big deal. A large percentage of people living in most parts of Europe in early 1945 would say they were lucky to be alive.

But then, unlike most of those people, Edward Bates had chosen this life. At that moment, he was part of a three-member team working on this mission, and the third member was a civilian appointed by the prime minister of England. And it was this person who was running the show.

Bates always tried not to care too much about his missions. As a field agent, his job was to follow orders, especially if they came directly from Number 10, such as this one, and to complete missions as well as he could. He tried to go about his job as dispassionately as possible. It made a lot of things simpler. Emotions complicated stuff and he did not like that, more so when it came to work.

But then, all plans do not work out the way we want.

After reaching the city and finding himself a place to stay—in the basement of a partially damaged building a little out of the city (he had paid the house owner handsomely)—he ran his fingers through his now-shoulder-length hair as he thought about how he was going to go about this operation. Also, he needed a haircut.

He decided the first thing to do was find people who knew about the painting and could possibly want to work together either for the love of the artwork or for the money. 'Basically, thieves or art lovers,' he chuckled to himself. The most obvious place to start his research was, of course, the Kaiser-Friedrich Museum.

As he walked through the city centre towards the museum, he looked around to see the buildings and people going about their everyday lives, and tried to imagine how the picture would change in a week.

His sources had told him that the curator of the museum had not been happy about moving the paintings to the salt mine, but had agreed reluctantly because there appeared no other way of hoping to save them. So, Bates thought it would be a good idea to start with talking to the curator himself. A lot of things would become simpler if he could get the curator on board.

Herr Bormann was not at his office when Bates came to the museum and sought an appointment with him. He was asked to come the next morning.

Bates and Herr Bormann met for the first time on the morning of January 10 at the latter's office.

The spy had, of course, given a false German name and identity when he had sought the appointment, and had stated the reason for wanting to see Herr Bormann as 'personal research'. He was now Tobias Kraus, a history teacher at a village some 10 kilometres down south along the Elbe.

'How may I help you, Herr Kraus?' the curator asked.

Bates started, not surprisingly, with a lie. 'Herr Bormann, I have visited the galleries in this museum numerous times in the past,' he said in impeccable German. The truth was that this was only his first visit to Magdeburg.

'That's good to know,' smiled Herr Bormann.

'So, it saddens me that you have had to pack away your collections and hide it in fear of British bombings,' said Bates.

'I can assure you my feelings on this matter are no different from yours,' said Herr Bormann. 'But the times we live in are such that we have to do so many things that, if given a choice, we would do them differently or not at all.'

The British spy seized the moment. 'If, Herr Bormann, you were given that choice, what would you do?'

'Excuse me?'

'I am sure you understand that hiding all those paintings in the salt mine may save them only from the bombings. When the Americans reach Stassfurt, and I say "when" deliberately instead of "if" because I know for certain they will, how will you protect them from plunder and arson? Do you have a plan for that situation? Those works of art are as vulnerable now as they were when they were on display here.'

'I know. I know.' Jonas stood up and started pacing back and forth. Edward kept quiet. After a minute, the curator said, 'Tell me the plan.'

'Herr Bormann, the plan is only to save one painting.'

'Just one? You must be joking. There are more than 400 paintings stored at the mine now!'

'This is a time of war. Resources are limited and we need to use whatever we have wisely. We can work together and save one painting, or let it be and wait for it to be destroyed or stolen,' Bates said.

'I suppose you already have a painting in mind?'

'I do,' said Bates.

When Herr Bormann realised that the painting on Bates' mind was #395, he did not take much time to agree to work with him.

'I am certainly not superstitious, but in this case, I am seriously tempted to consider it a sign. What are the chances of you coming to me with the proposal of saving one out of 400 paintings, and the one happens to be that which I care for the most?' said Herr Bormann, smiling. 'Now, I hope you will be kind enough to tell me your real name and who you are working for?'

The spy stood up and extended his hand. 'Edward Bates. I work for the British government. I am happy to have met you.'

Herr Bormann shook the hand with both of his. He had found a small light amid all the darkness.

While the curator found the resourceful friend he was looking for in Bates, the field agent found the perfect person who could help him carry out his mission.

After they had decided to work together, Bates asked, 'Do you have a solid basement in your house? One that could survive bombings?'

'We do, but we usually go over to the public bunkers when the sirens start blaring,' said Herr Bormann. 'You think we'll need one soon?'

'Yes. In six days,' said Bates.

'What are you saying? Where are you staying? We should warn everyone!'

'We will do no such thing, and you have heard nothing about a bombing on 16 January from me,' said the spy. 'I can take care of myself. You take care of yourself and your family.'

The curator stared at him.

Bates said, 'Is it okay if I go to your house and have a look at your basement now?'

'Yes, of course.' Herr Bormann was extremely disturbed.

He guided Bates out of his office, told a subordinate he had an urgent matter to attend to and would be back in an hour, and headed towards his house.

Claudia was trying to read a passage from an English book when she heard the knock on the door. Jonas had been teaching her to read and write in English over the past few months. 'It's the language of the future,' he had said.

She got up and peered through the peephole. They never opened the door without checking who it was. It was Herr Bormann, and there was someone else with him. She opened the door, smiled at her husband and looked at the stranger.

The clean-shaven man was of average height and had medium-length, wavy dark brown hair. She wanted to run her fingers through them and was surprised to find herself thinking that way.

'Bates, please meet my wife Claudia,' said Herr Bormann and then turning to Claudia, said, 'This is my friend; he needs to see our basement.'

'Hallo,' said Bates and gave her a polite smile. He didn't miss her lingering gaze on him.

The men went in and Herr Bormann showed him the basement, which Bates did not think was reliable for a bombing of the scale that was coming.

‘I don’t know if they will have time to sound the alarm. But if you go to the public bunker on your own, you will probably raise some eyebrows. So, I suggest you find a secure enough private basement and stay the night of 16 January there,’ said Bates.

He didn’t stay long. Before he left, Bates handed over a thick envelope to Herr Bormann. ‘I think this will be enough to start with. I will meet you again on the 12th morning,’ he said.

The hint of a smile played on both Bates and Claudia’s lips when their eyes met for the last time that day before the British spy left.

2012

IN SEARCH OF A DEAD DOCTOR

As the yellow taxi with a navy blue line across it snaked its way through the busy Central Avenue, she stared at what seemed like hundreds of battered public buses full of people on the road. Passengers sitting at the windows gawked at the curious young white woman looking out of the taxi's left rear window.

She could have taken the metro, for it would have been cheaper and quicker. But going through the streets in a new city was always exciting and she enjoyed it. She loved to hear the sounds and get a feel of the city's air. She waved back at a couple of school kids waving at her from the pavement.

Moreover, the public transport, including the taxis, in Kolkata is cheap by any standards.

A little later, the taxi passed by the Calcutta Medical College, a big gate on the left at the entrance to the street with the bust of a bearded man on top of it. She knew it was Tagore, a Bengali poet who had received the Nobel Prize in literature early in the twentieth century and who many Bengalis were obsessed with. She couldn't remember his first name, however.

Though she did not know it, a few minutes later they passed by Sonagachi, India's largest red light district.

It wasn't long before the old Ambassador taxi crossed a red temple bang in the middle of the onward and return lanes of Central Avenue. The car came to a stop a moment later by Jagat Mukherjee Park in the Raj Ballav Para locality of North Kolkata.

She got out, looked around and then looked at her phone screen. According to the map on her phone, she was on Madan Mohan Tala Street.

She didn't really have a plan on how to go about it. She had thought of getting on the street first and taking it from there. But that probably hadn't been the smartest way of going about it, she thought as she stood playing with her fingers and wondering what to do, as two street urchins kicked around a dirty red football a few feet away from her.

She noticed a middle-aged woman in a brown sari walking past with a rather large bag of groceries and decided to approach her.

'Hello. Could I have a minute please?' she called out to her from behind.

The woman stopped, turned around and smiled. The white woman whipped out a piece of paper from her sling bag and held it up for inspection. The woman placed her bag of groceries on the pavement, wiped her forehead with the end of her sari and peeked into the paper that the foreigner held.

'Daktar S-a-m-i-r K-u-m-a-r G-h-o-s-h,' the woman read with much difficulty. She looked towards the sky and appeared deep in thought. Then, she brought down her gaze to meet the foreigner's and said, 'No, no. Don't know.'

The white woman persisted. 'He used to live here in the 1940s. He is probably dead now, but his family might still be here. Do you think you might know them?'

'Don't know. Don't know,' said the woman, nodding her head. Then she picked up her bag and walked ahead.

Next, the visitor asked a shy young man, who understood English but smiled way too much and evidently hadn't heard of Dr Ghosh. In a few minutes, a small crowd had gathered with everyone trying to find out what she was looking for and everyone offering opinions on how she could find this person. She grew uncomfortable. This was the last thing she wanted—drawing attention to herself.

She decided her best bet was to get a local person to do the job for her.

She thanked them and quickly turned around to leave Madan Mohan Tala Street. She took a right on Central Avenue and walked till she reached Sovabazar Sutanuti Metro Station, and took the next south-bound train.

1945

THE PART-TIME TAILOR

On 11 January 1945, Herr Bormann arranged a meeting with a man who was known only as Al. He had a real name, of course. But hardly anyone apart from his mother knew or called him by the name of Alois.

The balding man was thin and had a three-day beard. Most people wouldn't give him a second thought if they saw him on the street, and that is just how he preferred it. Al liked to keep a low profile, but those who knew about his talent admitted that he was the best in the business.

Like everyone else, the two of them stood in the long queue in front of the local baker's shop and started talking in low voices. It would take them around two hours to enter the shop, and this was a good time to talk.

'I would like to employ your professional services,' whispered Herr Bormann.

'You mean you want a pair of trousers made, Herr Bormann?' grinned Al, who worked as an assistant to his mother, who ran a tailoring business. At least that was what most people thought he did. 'You need to come home and give us your measurements.'

'You know what I am talking about!' said Herr Bormann, feigning anger.

'Of course I do,' giggled Al. 'It's good to have a bit of humour in you in these grim times.'

'I agree,' said the curator. 'But it's only a matter of time before the work is destroyed, and we need to work fast.'

'This is not the kind of job where rushing produces the same result as when you have enough time.'

'I understand. Just however fast you can go about it,' said Herr Bormann, and told him what the painting was.

'I have seen it, of course. But I will need one colour photograph of the work. You know my fees, right?'

'Don't worry about it. Here's your advance,' Bormann passed an envelope over to him. 'The picture is inside as well.'

Al opened it, took a look inside, and stared back. 'Where did you get all this money?'

'Let's just say I have a friend and keep it at that. I want nothing less than perfection.'

'I guess you had your reasons for coming to me,' Al said, winking.

'I will wait and see if what they say about you is true.' Bormann did not smile. 'One day, the world will thank you for this.'

Al chuckled. 'Herr Bormann, I don't give a damn about the world.'

'One more thing.'

‘Yes?’

‘Do you happen to have a strong basement at your house?’

‘Why do you ask?’

At 8.30 the next morning, Al had a breakfast of bread and soup with his mother. He cursed under his breath because, with all that money Herr Bormann had given him, he could afford better food at that moment. Unfortunately, he had found nothing better the previous evening.

The small house they lived in was a little far from the bustling city centre—around a 50-minute walk from the Central Station.

Once they were done with breakfast, Al went to his room and locked the door. He then pushed aside his bed, and removed the worn-out, colourless carpet to reveal a 2x2-foot trapdoor. He opened it and climbed down the ladder into a 10x10-foot room stacked with canvases and colours and other painting materials. Two blank 49x45-centimetre canvases stood in the middle of the room. The only natural light entering the room was through the trapdoor, and Al needed the natural light to work. This is why he had several mirrors fixed along the stairways strategically to reflect light into the room, and this worked fairly well.

The colour photograph of the painting was already pinned on the wall behind the canvases.

Al clearly remembered the day his father had made the decision to build the basement. It was a Sunday, on 10 September 1939.

It was only the previous Sunday that Britain and France had declared war on Hitlerism. 3 September 1939 had been a day when many grave and inspiring messages were broadcast.

At 11.15 am, British prime minister Arthur Neville Chamberlain had spoken to his countrymen:

> *I am speaking to you from the cabinet room at 10 Downing Street. This morning, the British ambassador in Berlin handed the German government a final note, stating that, unless we heard from them by 11 o'clock that they were prepared at once to withdraw their troops from Poland, a state of war would exist between us.*
>
> *I have to tell you now that no such undertaking has been received, and that consequently this country is at war with Germany…*

Later that day, Chamberlain broadcast his message to the German common people in their own language.

> *German people! Your country and mine are now at war. Your government has bombed and invaded the free and independent state of Poland, which this country is honour-bound to defend.*
>
> *You are told by your government that you are fighting because Poland rejected your leader's offer and resorted to force. What are the facts? The so-called 'offer' was made to the Polish ambassador in Berlin on Thursday evening, two hours before the announcement by your government that it had been 'rejected'. So far from having been rejected, there had been no time even to consider it.*

'You may ask why Great Britain is concerned. We are concerned because we gave our word of honour to defend Poland against aggression. Why did we feel it necessary to pledge ourselves to defend this Eastern power when our interests lie in the West? The answer is—and I regret to have to say it—that nobody in this country any longer places any trust in your leader's word.

He gave his word that he would respect the Locarno Treaty. He broke it. He gave his word that he neither wished nor intended to annex Austria. He broke it. He declared that he would not incorporate the Czechs in the Reich. He did so. He gave his word after Munich that he had no further territorial demands in Europe. He broke it. He gave his word that he wanted no Polish provinces. He broke it. He has sworn to you for years that he was the mortal enemy of Bolshevism. He is now its ally.

Can you wonder his word is, for us, not worth the paper it is written on?

The German–Soviet Pact was a cynical volte-face, designed to shatter the Peace Front against aggression. This gamble failed. The Peace Front stands firm. Your leader is now sacrificing you, the German people, to the still-more monstrous gamble of a war, to extricate himself from the impossible position into which he had led himself and you.

In this war, we are not fighting against you, the German people, for whom we have no bitter feeling, but against a tyrannous and forsworn regime which has betrayed not only its own people but the whole of Western civilisation and all that you and we hold dear.

May God defend the right. *

'This is not good. They might not be fighting against us. But mark my words, we will be caught in the crossfire for sure,' Michael had said grimly.

'What should we do, Father?' Al had asked.

'We need to take care of ourselves. We will do what is in our control. The first thing is to start building a strong basement.'

'We will need people for that.'

'We will need no one. You and I will do it. And not a single soul outside this room needs to know we are building a basement. Do you understand?' he had said and looked at both Al and his mother. They both had nodded silently.

'And we need to work fast. We have to be ready when the war reaches our doorsteps,' Michael had said.

It was one thing to build a basement and quite another to build one secretly without anyone knowing. They had worked hard for two years and nearly had it complete. Then his father suddenly died and it was left to Al to finish the job. He did it in another year.

---

*[Source of Arthur Neville Chamberlain's speeches: *The Great Second War, A Standard History, Volume One*, The Waverley Book Company Ltd, in association with The Amalgamated Press Ltd, Farringdon Street, London ECA]

It was Michael who had taught him to paint. The man was a fine artist himself, but Al was a rare talent. People who were acquainted with his skills were of the opinion that no one could paint copies better than him. They said that if Al did not want you to, you would never be able to differentiate between his copy and the original. But the number of people who knew about his gift was tiny and it was only by a stroke of luck that Herr Bormann had got to know him through a common friend while restoring a damaged old painting.

Around January 1945, Al's life revolved around his mother and his paintings, which he worked on in secret inside the basement. Since being an artist was a risky job under Nazi rule, he was to the world his mother's assistant in her tailoring business.

Al stretched, had a good look at the painting pinned to the wall behind the two canvases, and started sketching. He needed to finish this job at the earliest.

2012

THE TASTE OF RUM

Tina hadn't been in Kolkata when Hannah and Eva were around, and so there hadn't been any complications. But of course, I had to tell her when she got back a day after they'd left. She wasn't happy, to say the least.

'I ask for this one thing and you can't even do that for me?'

I decided being quiet and avoiding her gaze was the best way to deal with the situation.

'Look at me, Neil! And don't play dumb!'

So that didn't work. 'Look, Tina, what has happened has happened. Fighting over spilt milk doesn't help.'

'What the hell are you talking about? Are you saying you had sex?'

Oh crap. That's what happens when I don't want to speak but have to. 'I didn't mean that. And no, we did not have sex! We didn't do anything!'

'I'd requested you to stay away from this Couchsurfing thing. Why did you do it again?' she asked, fighting tears.

I hate it when she does that. 'Tina...listen...don't cry. Well, I did it because...I don't know...because I wanted to...We'd had a talk about this, remember? But you backtracked!'

'That's because I thought I could handle it, but I realised I can't. It doesn't work that way! All that open relationship crap only works in theory!' Now she was shifting from teary to angry. I didn't know which version I preferred. None, actually.

'I know people in open relationships.'

'Then go have sex with them.' Tina stood up, fished out a couple of 100-rupee notes from her purse, placed them under a saucer on the table and left the cafe.

I tried calling her for the rest of the day and all of the next. She didn't pick up. We'd been together for close to a year but she'd never reacted this way before. I started wondering if we were still together.

I got a text message later that night. It was not from Tina.

Hi, Neil! My friends and I are organising a farewell party for Eva. Want to come to Delhi and join us? I know you like her;) Hannah.

This was certainly not a good time. But when I closed my eyes and thought of those dimples, it didn't take me long to decide what I was going to do. And well, in my defence, I wasn't even sure if Tina and I were still together.

I didn't call Tina any more and booked a flight to Delhi for the next day.

I got up late the next morning and remembered I was going to meet Eva later in the day. A smile had appeared on my lips automatically and I laughed out loud when I realised that.

But simultaneously, a tinge of guilt bugged me. That part, of course, concerned Tina. I tried convincing my mind we weren't together any more. In all the time we had been together, there had never been one instance when she had refused to take my calls two days in a row. Typically, it didn't take us more than a few hours to get over a fight.

This time was certainly different.

The more I thought about Tina, the more our good times together seemed to take a back seat and the unpleasant moments take the front row in my head. I didn't want to admit it to myself, but I understood I had started to fancy Eva way too much to be able to stay in the relationship with Tina.

Around noon, I took a long and hot shower and tried not to think about Tina. Unfortunately for me, we had spent far too much time together and that made it impossible to block those thoughts. I masturbated, more than anything else, in an effort to distract myself. I couldn't be sure how much that helped though.

I had a simple lunch of three rotis and chicken curry before leaving for the airport. Thirty minutes later, on the way to the airport, when my taxi was stuck at a traffic light on the Eastern Metropolitan Bypass, my mind was blank.

But when I slept on the flight, I only dreamt of dimples and uncle-glasses.

As a student, I had spent a few years in Delhi and consequently, I had enough friends in India's capital city. From the airport I went directly to my friend Arindam's place at Outram Lines in North Campus, where a number of colleges affiliated with the Delhi University are located.

It was good to catch up with an old friend and talk about old times. That momentarily took my mind off all the complicated stuff going on in my life. We walked over to our favourite hangout place in Hudson Lines, which is situated on the other side of the main road from Outram Lines. That was the place I used to go to for meals and generally hanging out with friends over chai when I lived in Delhi.

With a cup of hot, steaming milk tea in his hand, Arindam said, 'So, that's why this sudden trip? Just to meet this German girl?'

'Yes, man. I know I don't really know her that well. But I really like her.'

'I am not going to be judgemental, Neil. But what about your girlfriend?'

'I don't know,' I mumbled, not even looking at the cup of tea sitting on the same raised platform our bums were resting on. 'If there's a hell, Arindam, I know I am going to roast in it.'

'I'm no good at giving advice on such complicated matters. Do you want to have a chicken roll from the shop around the corner? They're sure not as good as the ones in Kolkata, but they are not too bad either,' said Arindam, to whom food was the solution to most problems in the world. And if you think about it, it actually is.

We did have the chicken rolls and I had to agree—they weren't bad at all, other than the fact that they cost double of what they'd have in Kolkata. But then, Delhi was by far a costlier city.

While we walked back to Arindam's place, I bought a bottle of Old Monk for the party, especially because both Eva and Hannah loved it. The venue wasn't too far from his place. I said goodbye to my friend and took an autorickshaw to my destination.

The party was taking place at the apartment of a French guy, who was also here to teach at Delhi University for a few months. When I reached around 9.30 that night with my bottle of Old Monk, Hannah opened the door and took me to Eva, who was chatting with a few people on the sofa. The moment I saw her, all thoughts about Tina evaporated from my mind just like that.

'Oh my God! What are you doing here, Neil?' She came over and gave me a tight hug.

I loved the feeling of her breasts against my chest and immediately cursed myself for thinking sexually all the time. Then I consoled myself again with the excuse that the average man thinks of sex once every four minutes.

She looked into my eyes through her gold-rimmed spectacles and said, 'It's good to see you again!'

'It's good to see you, too! This was Hannah's idea and I liked it.'

I was one of the two Indians at the party. The other Indian guy was engaged to a German girl, who was also there. Then there was a tall French girl, a British guy, the French man whose place this was, and his father, who was visiting him.

All the food and drinks were in the kitchen, from where you had to help yourself.

I made myself a drink and looked around.

The flat, which was in North Delhi's Kamla Nagar, had a medium-sized common room, where most of the people were sitting. The owner of the place, Nick, was sitting at the table and playing music on a laptop. By owner, I of course mean the person who was renting the place and living there at that point. Nick's father, who had cooked some rice and veggies for us, was talking to Maria, the fiancée of the other Indian guy, Arun, on the other side of the table.

On the opposite side of the room were the sofas where Eva was chatting animatedly with Arun, while Hannah was out on the balcony with the British guy, Adrian, who I later got to know was her boyfriend. The tall French girl was sitting alone on the end of a sofa and checking her phone. Since she was the only one not talking to someone, I went and sat next to her. 'Hi, I'm Neil.'

'Caroline.'

Caroline was from Normandy and I was fascinated with her stories of Cany-Barville, the commune near the English Channel, where her parents' home was. It sounded picture-perfect.

'If you come to France, you should come and stay at my parents' place. I'm sure they will love having you over, and I could show you around,' she said. 'I think you will like it.'

'Thank you! I will let you know for sure if I am around.'

I went to refill my glass and came back to find Caroline talking with Arun and Eva, who smiled at me. I smiled back and sat beside her.

'Did you just come to Delhi to attend my farewell party?' she whispered to me.

'Yes. Hannah texted and said they were organising this thing and asked if I wanted to come.'

'And you said yes?'

'Yes!'

'Thank you. You're sweet. But seriously, Neil, didn't you say you have a girlfriend? Does she know?'

'Well, she has not been picking up my calls and I don't even know if we are still together.'

'Okay,' she said, and an awkward silence followed.

We stared ahead for a while watching the others. I noticed after a while that Eva's glass was empty and I offered to get her a new drink. She said she'd do it herself and stood up and headed to the kitchen. I accompanied her. She saw the bottle of Old Monk there and smiled.

'I didn't know we had Old Monk here! Who brought this one?' she said and looked at me. 'Of course it's you,' she said and giggled.

'Well, yeah,' I said.

She poured herself a drink and we headed back to the sofa.

She spoke once we were seated. 'Look, Neil, you're nice. But let's not rush into something. First, figure out what's happening between you and your girlfriend.'

'Yeah.'

'And you should come to Berlin again. You now have one more friend there!'

'Yeah,' I said quietly and mentally made a note that I needed to plan my fifth visit to the city soon.

'What?'

'I like you, Eva,' I said quietly.

She looked at Nick, who was playing 'Careless Whisper'. 'Want to dance?'

She had just said we should not rush into something—then why would she ask me to dance? That came to my head for sure, but I didn't want to dwell on it. The dimples overshadowed all reasonable things in my head at that point.

We danced slow. After a few minutes, she rested her head on my shoulder. Arun and Maria were dancing too. Nick followed up with the hopelessly romantic 'Annie's Song'. His father sat with a drink on the sofa in a deep conversation with Caroline. I couldn't see Hannah and Adrian anywhere.

'You know, Neil…'

I came back to reality.

'If I drink too much at a party, the next day, I can often not remember what happened the previous night.'

'Have you had too much to drink tonight?' I asked, laughing loudly.

'I'm certainly going in the right direction.' We both burst into giggles.

I wanted to kiss her so bad. I gave her a peck on the right dimple.

'Let's not kiss tonight, Neil. If she's still your girlfriend, she does have a right to know what's happening here.'

'I'll try calling her right now.'

'You most certainly will not. It is 2.30 in the morning and you are drunk. Not the perfect setting for an important discussion.'

'I guess you're right.' I put my arms around her in a tight hug. I didn't want the moment to end.

'Would you want to tell me what the problem is between you and your girlfriend?'

I told her everything. Right from our open relationship plan to the Couchsurfing incident and Tina's reaction to it.

'So, you'd be perfectly okay if she did something like that?'

'My perception of loyalty is a little different from most people. I wouldn't consider Tina disloyal if she had sex with someone. I'd consider her disloyal only if she hid the fact from me.'

'I have to say you are pretty broad-minded. Open relationships aren't that common even in Germany.'

'I know so many people who are cheating on their partners in the sense that they are hiding stuff. So, if I could be in an open relationship, I think it would be quite a healthy one.'

'Hmm. That's one way of looking at it.'

I had to leave early the next morning, for my flight was at 7.20 am. Eva's flight was later in the night. I hadn't had any sleep and was a little hung-over from all that rum. Hannah was asleep by Adrian on a sofa and I didn't want to wake her up. Eva hadn't slept.

Before I left, we hugged. I didn't want to let go and felt a little uncomfortable realising my eyes were moist.

'You've got to let me go now,' she said.

I pulled back.

Then she said, 'I've given it some thought...I'm sure we'll meet again. But what if we don't?'

I looked into her eyes. 'Given what some thought?'

'This,' she said, and kissed me on the lips.

She tasted of rum.

2012

THE STRANGER WITH A HUNDRED QUESTIONS

The call came at 7.25 am.

'Did I wake you up?'

'Uh huh. Who is this?'

'Sarkar from the agency in Kolkata.'

She sat up. 'Yes?'

'We have found the family. They sold their North-Kolkata property many years ago and now live at Jodhpur Park in South Kolkata. Do you want the details now?'

She was wide awake now. 'Hold on a minute,' she said and got out of bed to find her bag, from where she dug out a small writing pad and a pen. 'Tell me.'

The conversation lasted two more minutes. Then she made a call to Sankar Ghosh, a neurologist who lived in Jodhpur Park. Twenty minutes later, she was in a cab headed for the airport. When her flight to Kolkata was cruising at 32,000 feet, she pulled out the letter from her bag and read it again.

My dear Claudia,

I hope this letter finds you well. It is highly unprofessional of me to be writing to you this way. But I know in my heart that I will not survive this illness and I don't really care about professionalism at this moment.

I am very sorry about Herr Bormann's death. He was a good man and I feel terribly guilty of having fallen in love with his wife. But that is how it is and I cannot change it. You cannot instruct your heart what to do all the time.

I am writing to you from my hospital bed in Calcutta. I have made friends with a native doctor called Samir Kumar Ghosh, who is taking care of me. He stays at Madan Mohan Tala Street and has even invited me to visit his family when I get well. He is doing his best, I am sure. I have been told he is among the best doctors in Calcutta, but I don't think he will be able to save me on this occasion. Something is very, very wrong inside me and I can feel it.

I wish I could see you, my love.

Yours forever,
Edward Bates
Calcutta,
15 June 1945

'Too many details about the doctor in a love letter from a dying man,' she told herself once more.

'What exactly is it that you want?'

'I intend to find out if the painting survived.'

'What will you do if you find it still exists?'

'I am not sure. But I think it would be nice if it returned to the Magdeburg gallery. But it's just important for me to know what happened. You know why.'

The 60-year-old doctor picked up the cup of tea from the centre table. Her eyes followed his cup, but she didn't pick up the one offered to her. *How much does he know?*

'I can understand your genuine interest in this painting from the fact that you came all the way to Kolkata, found me out and are sitting here right now. However, all I know about you is what you have told me.'

'You can check my background if you want, sir. And I have shown you the letter.'

'That you have. But you don't have much time for stories, do you? Your flight back is in a few hours from now.'

'I will take a later flight if need be. This is what I came to India for.'

'Hmm. And you still don't know what painting it is, do you?'

'No, sir.'

'The information I have is what I've heard from my father, who had heard it from his father. All of it might not be factually accurate and I don't think it's something that will excite you too much.'

'I would still be interested to hear it, sir. Would you please tell me which painting this was?' She held her breath.

The kind doctor told her. 'So you see why it would cause quite a furore in the art world if it surfaced today,' he added.

'Yes, sir.'

'My grandfather was a renowned doctor. My father and I followed in his footsteps. My daughter decided to be an investment banker, though. But let me not divert. The reputation of my grandfather, Samir Kumar Ghosh, was so great that the British entrusted him with treating their top officers. Bates was one of them.'

'When did he arrive in India?'

'Bates came under my grandfather's care within three days of his arrival in India, which was some time in the middle of 1945. He had peritonitis. During the short time he was under Grandfather's treatment, a British official came time and again and asked him all sorts of questions regarding the painting. At least, that is what my grandfather thought happened behind closed doors. This, despite being told that Bates needed rest and not high blood pressure from excitement.'

'What happened then?'

'On the fourth day, he was doing no better and the officer came again. No one was allowed in the private room when the two talked. But this time, there were a lot of raised voices and cursing and Samir intervened. He told the officer that Bates was his patient and he would not allow this. The officer left. Then Samir and Bates had a conversation.'

The girl sat up straight. It appeared he was finally getting to the point.

'Bates told him he did not feel well and he was beginning to be unsure if he was ever going to return to England. Samir asked him what the matter was and why he was so disturbed. He was just making conversation, since the patient seemed so miserable. Surprisingly, Bates opened up. Perhaps, it was Bates' realisation that he was dying, and he did not want the information to die with him.'

'And this information was about the painting?' She was sitting up straight on the sofa.

'The order had come from Number 10, he said.' The doctor's half-finished cup of tea had turned cold on the centre table. The visitor's cup was still untouched.

'Is that 10 Downing Street?' she whispered.

'Yes. Bates worked with the SIS. Someone at Number 10 had seen this painting at some point and had been fascinated by it. This person wanted to save it at any cost. Bates said this person did not necessarily have to be Churchill, but could have been someone close to him to have influence enough to commission this mission. At that point, Magdeburg was being bombed left and right and this influential person didn't want this painting to be destroyed.'

'The SIS is MI6, right?' She was at the edge of her seat.

'Of course. James Bond trained under Bates,' the doctor said and laughed at his own joke.

The girl smiled politely.

The doctor continued, 'Bates went to Magdeburg and made friends with the curator of the museum. The curator told Bates that he himself was a big admirer of the artist and would be happy to do it. They both chalked out a plan.'

'Jonas Bormann.'

'Excuse me?'

'That was the curator's name,' she said quietly.

'Oh. So, Jonas and Bates decided to have a copy made of the painting and replace the original at the earliest. Bates would take care of the original till the end of the war and would ensure it returned to the gallery afterwards.'

Mrs Ivy Ghosh came into the room at this point. 'Come, you two. Lunch is waiting.'

'Yes, you look positively tired and hungry to me. I'll tell you the rest after lunch,' said the doctor and stood up.

She got up reluctantly and followed the doctor to the dining table. Sankar and his family had been kind and understanding to a random stranger with a hundred questions. She could wait a little more.

1945

THE FOUR SURVIVORS

As surprising as it may have seemed, Adolf Hitler rarely stayed in Berlin, capital of the Großdeutsches Reich, for extended periods. But this time, it was different. On 15 January 1945, when he returned to Berlin from his Western Front capital, he found the relentless bombing raids by the Red Army too much to handle.

Consequently, he had little choice but to enter the underground Führerbunker on 16 January. The Führer was to stay there for 105 days straight till he would commit suicide with his partner and later wife, Eva Braun.

Herr Bormann and Claudia knocked on Al's door at 10 the same morning Hitler descended into his bunker-cum-headquarters. Al's mother welcomed them in and had them sit at the dining table. She then knocked on her son's door and told him he had visitors. Five minutes later, the part-time tailor opened the door of his room and came out.

'When exactly does your friend expect it to start?' he said as he walked to join the couple at the table.

'In the evening. But I think we should go down after lunch just to be safe,' said Herr Bormann.

'We will do that, then. But if we are really sure that the attack is happening, shouldn't we tell people?'

'Who do you want to tell? The entire town? Then if it actually happens, they'd ask you how you knew and when you don't want to say that, they'll brand you a British spy and kill you. And if it doesn't happen they'll call you a liar and probably kill you anyway,' said Herr Bormann, repeating the reasons Bates had given him as to why he should not tell anyone about the bombing.

Al kept quiet.

Herr Bormann continued, 'He asked me not to tell a soul and only to take care of the people closest to me. I really don't have many friends or family here and I know you don't, too. So, I'm just here with my wife. But the sirens will blare as usual, of course.'

'So the only reason he is trying to save us is because we are working for him?'

'Yes, but I would say it's a little bigger than that. Perhaps it is better if you did not know all the details,' said Herr Bormann.

'You are right. I don't really want to know too many details. I take a job, do it well and that's that. That is the way to go about it. Save yourself first in the time of war,' said Al. The last part he mumbled to himself.

The four had an early lunch, closed all doors and windows tight, filed into Al's room and climbed down into his studio. Al came last and shut the trap door behind him. The dark little room had been lit up by two lamps. Al had stashed all his painting equipment on the other side of the room. He didn't want them to catch fire from the lamps.

'Is there a passage for air to get into this place? We are four people and there are two lamps burning,' said Herr Bormann.

'One, two and three,' said Al, pointing at three pipes that ended at three corners of the ceiling. 'They bring in air from three different points just in case one gets blocked for some reason.'

'That is very good. This looks like a well-planned construction,' the curator said.

'My father and I built it from scratch over several years,' said Al proudly. 'But I am a little scared for it tonight.'

'Thanks for letting us stay here,' Claudia said and looked at Al's mother, who smiled in reply.

The four sat there for hours, talking of random things, cursing Hitler, cursing the Soviets, cursing the war and cursing the Brits for coming to bomb the city. But the bombs never came. Al grew impatient around 8 pm.

'Are you sure they're coming?'

'From what I know, they are coming this evening. I don't have the exact time. But from what my friend said, they definitely are coming. It's in his interest that we live. So, I don't think he would be feeding us crap. He has nothing to gain from it.'

When the air-raid sirens finally started blaring at 9.28 pm, the first bomb had already detonated. The attack was nothing like Magdeburg had seen before. For 39 minutes,

371 planes of the Royal Air Force carpet-bombed the central part of the city. The four sat as still as they could, holding their breaths and each other's hands. Al's mother wept silently and the artist kept looking at his painting equipment every now and then to make sure they were okay. They put the lamps off in case the basement was damaged and the fire caught somehow. Initially, Herr Bormann tried to count the blasts in his head, but in a while he lost track. They jumped when a bomb dropped somewhere near and the ground trembled and the house shook. Beads of sweat flowed down their faces despite the January cold. They knew the house had suffered damage, but it was hard to understand exactly how much, from 10 feet below the ground.

The attack reduced Magdeburg to a mass of rubble. The flattened city centre burned for days after the bombing ended. In those 39 minutes of bombing, 2,500 people died, 11,000 were injured and 190,000 were rendered homeless.

The four people huddling in the 10x10-foot underground room survived.

The next morning, when they climbed out of the hole and witnessed with their eyes the destruction all around, the three of them in the know said a silent thank you to a certain painter who had put a bullet through his own chest and died young 55 years ago.

2012

CALLING IT QUITS

In the middle of 2011, I had met Tina on OkCupid.

We'd chatted regularly for a week or so before exchanging numbers and finally meeting up after three weeks. We did not delete our accounts on the website even though we'd decided to be in a relationship.

At that point, I'd thought she was the coolest girlfriend ever. Both of us had even gone on a few harmless dates afterwards and everything was going perfectly until the Couchsurfing incident.

I seriously didn't understand what cracked her up, and the relationship was getting a little suffocating for me. I wanted to do what I wanted to do and also, I did not want to hide the fact from her. I was still in love with her (even though I was infatuated/in love/not-sure-what with Eva).

I tried calling her again after I got back. This time she picked up.

'I want to see you, Tina. Will you meet me on Sunday?'

'Where?'

'Barista at Park Street around 5 pm?'

So far so good. I intended to tell her everything and see how she reacted. This was how it was supposed to be between us. No secrets. No regrets.

She was right on time.

'Hi,' she said.

'Hi.'

This was awkward.

'What do you want to say?'

'Why didn't you take my calls?'

'You know why. What's that you wanted to say?'

'You'd never reacted this way before. I thought you were going to break up or something.'

'Hmm.'

That was an unexpected reaction. Was she really looking to break up? Should I have been happy or should I have been sad? She was confusing me to no end. She was acting so cool.

'What I wanted to tell you is: I went to Delhi on Friday… to attend Eva's farewell party.'

'Oh.'

'Oh? That's all you're going to say?'

'Neil, I know I couldn't make this your ideal relationship. I thought I'd be able to do that.'

'I thought it was your idea of an ideal relationship too.'

'Yes. I guess you're right. But how'd I know then that I wouldn't be able to handle it at some point?'

'I don't blame you, Tina.'

'I guess it's best if we call it quits.'

It wasn't that I wasn't expecting something like this. Yet, I didn't feel good doing this. Quietly, I said, 'I guess.'

'Now go screw your German bitch in peace,' she said through clenched teeth.

I had not expected that. But I was happy she said it. All my guilt disappeared in one instant. I didn't reply. I stood up, fished out my share of the bill, placed the notes on the table, and headed for the door. While walking out, I saw Tina's head buried in her palms through the corner of my eyes.

Beyond was a good place to work at. It was a feature service that focused mostly on travel and allied stories. We were just six people on the rolls but we had a lot of freelancers working for us. We didn't really have an office. While Shreya and I worked out of Kolkata, Priyanka was based in Mumbai, Prasanta in Bangkok, Judy in Vancouver and Sree in London. Apart from Shreya, Priyanka and me, everyone had regular jobs.

We catered to publications based both in India and abroad, and while Priyanka looked after the marketing, the rest of us concentrated on the writing part. Shreya, who owned the company, also was our tech girl and took care of the website. Apart from writing, I also edited the stories filed by our freelancers. With the help of these freelancers, *Beyond* churned out some 50 to 60 feature stories a month. Our website also generated some revenue.

We were not making millions, but certainly enough to get by. We worked at our pace, set our own deadlines and delivered. *Beyond* didn't care if you were in town or not as long as you finished your assignments on time. All of us felt *Beyond* was ours and we toiled away to make it work. Just two years in, with our marketing girl's impressive skills, we were doing fairly well and often went on trips.

I filed a 1,000-word story on the ambience of the streets of Delhi University's North Campus on the night of my official breakup with Tina.

A Manipuri girl walks hand in hand with a turbaned Punjabi guy who's trying to portray to her the beauty of a slab of butter sliding down a hot aloo paratha.

It is midnight and I realise Delhi is not just about hate.

That's how my story began.

I got a call from Shreya on Monday morning. 'Good story, Neil! I love the beginning! Did you just go to Delhi or is this from an old trip?'

'Thanks. I was there a couple of days ago.'

'Tina and you?'

'Just me. Actually we broke up yesterday.'

'What! Are you okay?'

'Yes, I am fine. But thanks for asking.'

'It seems a breakup brings out the best of the writer in you. Take care, Neil. I'll see you around.'

I wrote furiously over the next few weeks, rarely leaving home.

1945

THE FIRST FIRE

Though neither of them lived in the city centre and their houses were situated a little away from the periphery of the area where the carpet bombing had taken place, it was nothing short of a miracle that the houses of both Al and Herr Bormann were largely unaffected by the air attack of 16 January 1945. Even more surprising was the fact that the Kaiser-Friedrich Museum stood amid the rubble following the attack. The museum would only be damaged on 15 February by targeted bombing by British and American aircrafts.

Al's house had a damaged window and he and Herr Bormann managed to patch it up in a couple of hours. The Bormanns stayed at Al's place for the rest of the week, till the fires in the city had been doused and life could start limping back.

The curator paid a few visits to the museum and the two of them eventually returned to their house on the morning of

22 January because Bates had sent word to Herr Bormann that he would meet him there for lunch that day. He had also promised to bring food.

Bates came two hours after they had reached home and hugged both of them. The hug with Claudia lasted a wee bit longer and the two separated immediately when they realised this. He had brought meat and bread and also a bottle of water, which they shared. Over lunch, the curator and his wife told the spy how they had spent that fateful evening.

When Herr Bormann went to the toilet that evening, Bates and Claudia kissed for the first time.

'The Allies are closing in on Magdeburg and Stassfurt. They should be here soon,' said Bates.

'But that's a good thing, right?' said Herr Bormann.

'Probably, but what I am worried about is the arson and looting right after they take over.'

'I know the paintings are not safe in the mine at all.' Herr Bormann looked worried.

'Absolutely not! Nothing is safe anywhere.'

'I should tell the painter to hurry up. But then, I have told that to him a hundred times already.'

Bates nodded his head. 'He's doing his best, I am sure.'

'He is.'

'When does he expect to finish?'

'Not before April.'

'What? You hadn't told that me it'd be that late!'

'You never asked for a specific date. Bates, please understand it's technical and such a job takes time. I think even three months is quick for this kind of work by any standards. He is not just making a new painting; he is creating one that looks exactly the same as another one that was painted several years ago,' Herr Bormann said.

'I understand. But please convey to him that if we don't finish this as early as possible, we won't have a painting to save. Ideally, we should do it on the first day of the arrival of the American or British troops to Stassfurt,' said Bates, deep in thought.

'I will talk to him again about this,' said Herr Bormann.

The Americans got into Stassfurt on 12 April 1945, and the first fire caught in the mine the same day. That was when Bates got paranoid and rushed to Herr Bormann's house.

Claudia opened the door.

'Mr Bates! Come on in. You look positively harried. What's wrong?'

'Where's Herr Bormann? I need to see him immediately.'

'He'd said he was going to Al's place.'

'Oh. When is he getting back?'

'I'm not sure. He left not long before you arrived. So, I suppose not before another hour or so. Would you like a drink?'

'Yes, please.'

Claudia poured the alcohol in a glass and handed it over to Bates, who sat at the table. Bates took it and said, 'Why don't you pour yourself one too?'

Claudia did so and joined him. For five minutes they sat in silence, interrupted intermittently by the sound of the glass against the table after each sip. Finally, she said, 'Mr Bates, what's wrong?'

'I honestly think it will be better if I just talked to Herr Bormann directly.'

'All right.'

Another few minutes of silence followed. Then she said, 'Do you want to talk about what happened the other day?'

'I...I don't know,' Bates stammered.

'What's wrong? Do you feel guilty?'

'I guess...yes. Actually yes, I do,' he said, avoiding Claudia's eyes. Then he downed the rest of his drink.

Claudia walked up next to Bates to refill his glass. 'Let me...' she began.

'No, no. Let me get this,' he said, stood up suddenly and kept his hands on Claudia's to stop her from picking up his glass.

The touch heightened the tension already in the air. They stood silently looking into each other's eyes, with Bates swallowing a gulp of air and Claudia's lips quivering.

Then, he closed his eyes and brought his mouth close to hers. She reciprocated.

The kisses were short and gentle first before they became longer and more intense. The two held each other and kissed for several minutes before Bates lowered his head and started kissing below her ears, then her neck and collarbone. He then brought his left hand that had been holding her waist and cupped her breast through the blouse. She drew in a sharp breath. Bates lifted his lips from her collarbone and looked into her eyes. She smiled uncertainly and they kissed again.

The two took their time and helped each other out of their clothes. The lovemaking was slow and patient. Neither was in a hurry as they both knew they had time. Bates loved the little noises Claudia made as they kissed.

After some 20 minutes, when they lay spent in each other's arms on the floor, Bates decided he was in love with this woman. But his feeling of guilt at having betrayed Herr Bormann was overpowering.

From the disturbed look on his face, Claudia understood how he felt. She leaned her face towards his and said, 'Ed, listen to me. I am not proud of what I have done, either. But we have at least been honest to ourselves. We did what we wanted to do. For all you know, we could be dead by tonight.'

Bates gave her a smile that did not light up his eyes. 'Yes,' he said and kissed Claudia's cheek. 'But I still hate myself.'

'No, Ed...'

'And you know what's worse?' he said as he got back into his clothes. 'I am hopelessly in love with you.'

When Bates got ready to leave, Claudia said, 'Aren't you going to wait for Jonas to come back?'

'I don't think I can look him in the eye at this moment. And he'd suspect something was amiss if we behaved awkwardly in front of him. Could you please tell him to meet me on the eastern side of the Magdeburger Dom at six in the evening?'

'I will do that,' she said.

Bates walked to the door and opened it to leave. But he hesitated, before closing it and coming back to Claudia. They hugged tightly. 'Yes, I hate myself for it, but I do love you, Claudia,' he said in her ear, and left.

At six, Bates saw Herr Bormann walking towards him with brisk steps. He took two deep breaths. He had to be professional. He had a job to finish and emotions had no place here.

'How much longer? If you can't convince this painter, let me go and talk to him,' he said without introduction as soon as the curator as within earshot.

'I can assure you, Bates, that the man is doing his best. It'll be ready soon.'

'Herr Bormann, I have told you earlier that if we do not do this quickly enough, the whole point of everything we have done till date is lost. I saved your lives for this!' he nearly screamed.

'I'd know that even if you hadn't made it this apparent. I thought we'd become friends too.'

'I'm sorry. I shouldn't have said that,' said Edward quietly. Now, he started feeling doubly bad. 'But there's pressure from Number 10 and the situation is getting on my nerves.'

'Hmm.'

'You need to give me a date, Jonas.'

'Date? Let's say two weeks?'

'That's too long a time. It has to be earlier! There has been a fire at the mines already and some artworks have already been destroyed. At this point I am not even sure if #395 survives!'

'What are you saying?'

'Exactly what you hear. I am heading out to Stassfurt in an hour to find out as much as I can. But please, *please* have the painting completed at the earliest.'

‘I will pay the artist a visit right now.’

Bates turned and started to walk away. But then he turned back and came up to Herr Bormann again and held his hand. ‘I consider you my friend, Jonas. Have no doubts about that.’

‘Thank you, Bates. You, too, should understand that my love for the painting is no less than yours. If I thought this man could have done it earlier and was wasting our time, I would have told you so. But I understand this kind of work, and people will identify a hurriedly done effort in two minutes, and that would defeat the entire purpose of everything we are doing.’

Bates nodded silently and the two men walked away in opposite directions.

1945

A COPY OF THE MASTERPIECE

In the second week of April, the Americans had reached the other side of the Elbe, and Magdeburg was among the only major cities left for the Allies to capture before they marched to Berlin.

On the morning of 16 April, the American 120th Infantry informed the Germans of its plan to attack and capture Magdeburg. By midday, attempts to negotiate with the German commanding general, Lt Gen. Regener, and to receive a surrender of the city, failed.

Consequently, the Americans decided to attack the city, which appeared the only place on the western side of the Elbe river to have some form of organised defence at that time. On 17 April at 11.45 am, they began air strikes on the city, the centre of which was nothing more than an open stretch full of rubble by then. The strikes continued intermittently for three-and-a-half hours before the infantry moved in. The defence preparations of the Germans were only partially complete when the Americans arrived and found half-dug trenches. The only major trouble that they faced was from snipers, who were practically everywhere. The Americans called more men over, and though it took time to search every nook and corner of the ruined buildings, they managed to overcome this problem.

The attackers had anticipated some trouble from civilians, but most of them were either in bomb shelters because of the frequent attacks on the city lately, and others remained hidden in their basements. As the day progressed, some civilians began to come out of their houses out of curiosity but that interfered with the attack only a little bit. Not long afterwards, a number of people were out and about, most of them going to buy stuff at the food shops. Shortly after midday on 18 April, the Americans completely captured the city.

Things became a little simpler for Bates now that the Americans were in possession of both Magdeburg and Stassfurt. But after networking with the American troops, what he heard didn't make him happy at all. If the painter did not manage to finish his work on time, all the time, effort and money would go down the drain.

At the meeting with a delegation of partisans at the palace of Milan's cardinal, Alfredo Schuster, Benito Mussolini learnt that the Nazis were negotiating an unconditional surrender behind his back.

To say he was furious was an understatement. But underneath all that anger was naked fear—the fear of a horrible death. He stormed out of the palace and attempted to flee the country with his mistress Clara Petacci.

On 12 April 1945, the partisans stopped the convoy in which the 61-year-old dictator and his 33-year-old mistress were trying to escape, along with some of their Fascist supporters.

Before the first light on 29 April the bullet-ridden bodies of the former dictator, his mistress and of his supporters were transported to Milan in a truck and dumped at Piazzale Loreto.

Al finished the job that day.

Over the last week or so, he had left his work to bake under a powerful lamp to age it 50 years. And just baking would not do. Al was the best because of the delicate tricks he had up his sleeves. He took care to ensure not to age the colours too much.

Al and Herr Bormann managed to meet that evening.

'It's done. I hope you are able to carry out the next part of your plan smoothly.'

'Yes. I can't thank you enough. Make sure you clean your studio of all evidence. Where is the photograph?'

'I burnt it. What happens to the original?'

'I believe all this fighting and chaos will end soon. I hope to actually find it, and will keep it somewhere safe till the situation gets better. I just can't bear to see this one burn.'

'If you're ever going to sell it, Herr Bormann, I want half of what you make.'

'I am not an art thief, Al. I will not sell it.'

'So be it, then. Do what you have to do as soon as possible. Every moment is precious. And I am sorry I could not finish earlier. You know I would have done it if I could,' said Al and fished out a foot-and-a-half-long cylindrical package from inside his coat. 'Here you are.'

'I can't believe you've been walking around with this!'

'I hope you have a safe place for the original.'

'I do. So how do I know which the original is?'

'Herr Bormann, do you believe size matters?' Al grinned.

Herr Bormann smiled. 'I am not sure I can guess where you are going with this.'

Al chuckled and proceeded to explain.

After a few minutes, both left. While Herr Bormann went directly in the direction of the now-damaged museum, Al walked home.

Bates met Herr Bormann in front of the museum. When Herr Bormann told him the work was complete, to say Bates was relieved would have been an understatement.

'There is going to be a fire at the Stassfurt mine the day after tomorrow. We are going to conduct the switch in that confusion. It will be risky and we have to be quick. But the Americans have agreed to give us this window,' said Bates.

'Where do we meet?'

'Meet me here at noon tomorrow. The truck leaves at 1 pm. We will spend the night at a camp there and enter the mines on the 30th morning.'

'We will need some time. I have to get the painting off the frame and put this in.'

'How much time do you need?'

'Around 30 minutes,' said Herr Bormann.

‘But why do you need so much time when that painting is going to be destroyed?’

‘Are you sure of that? Because if it’s saved by some fluke, we would want people to think it was the original, right?’

‘Right. We’ve just got to work as quickly as we can. See you at noon tomorrow.’

1945

A WEDDING AND A DEATH

In the early hours of 29 April, Walther Wagner, a minor official in the Großdeutsches Reich government, married Adolf Hilter and his long-time mistress Eva Braun inside the Führerbunker even as the Soviet troops closed in on the Reichstag and Chancellery.

The Führer then retired to a room with his secretary Traudl Junge and dictated to him his last will and testament.

The same day, Al had an afternoon snack of some delicious sausages that he had managed to procure after much legwork and spending a fair amount of cash. Of course, he didn't mind spending all that money, because he had quite a bit of it in hand to spend.

Herr Bormann, bless his soul, had paid him well, he thought, as he drained his sixth drink.

The sky was still bright and Al suddenly had a desire to paint. With the help of the mirrors, he would still have good light in his studio for at least three hours. He went into his room and pushed aside his bed. His head suddenly felt a little odd. He held the wall to support himself and stood still for a minute before removing the carpet and opening the 2x2-foot trapdoor. He then proceeded to climb down the ladder.

As he leaned to grab the edge of the opening before placing his feet on the ladder steps to climb down, his drunken brain misjudged the distance. He ended up grabbing nothing but thin air, lost his balance, and fell head first down the trapdoor.

Al's mother only found his lifeless body the next morning.

1945

THE SECOND FIRE

On 30 April, the Führer held his last staff meeting, wherein he was informed that the advancing Soviet forces were only a few blocks away.

Hitler listened to all the negative developments without comment. He had accepted the fact that his time had come. All he was concerned about at that moment was that his body should not meet the same fate as Benito Mussolini's once he had killed himself. He had given specific orders to Martin Bormann to ensure that it did not happen.

Once the goodbyes with his staff members were done, Hitler and his wife entered their private room. Eva shut the door, but did not latch it. The couple did not want Martin Bormann, the executer of the Führer's last will and testament, to have much trouble retrieving their bodies once they were dead. He had been instructed to burn them at the earliest.

Once inside, the couple kissed. Then they sat beside each other on the sofa. Hitler put his left hand into his pocket and brought out two capsules of cyanide and handed one over to his wife. Both of them held the capsules in their hands as they looked into each other's eyes and kissed for the last time.

Hitler held his 7.65 mm Walther pistol in his right hand as the couple took the capsules. He did not want to take any chances. He brought the gun up to his right temple and fired.

Unaware of the developments at the Führerbunker, around 200 kilometres away the same day, Jonas Bormann and Edward Bates descended 460 metres into the Stassfurt salt mine to switch painting #395. The fire caught 15 minutes later, spread quickly and assumed alarming proportions. A number of people died, and hundreds of artworks were damaged and lost.

After the fire was put out, they could only identify Herr Bormann's burnt body from the silver wedding ring on his finger.

Painting #395, better known to the world as Vincent van Gogh's masterpiece, *The Painter on the Road to Tarascon*, was destroyed in the same fire.

Or so the world thought.

2012

WHAT THE CURATOR DID

'Jonas took the responsibility to get a copy made because he told Bates that he knew someone who could help,' the doctor resumed his story after lunch.

The meal was heavy and it made the young woman feel sleepy. But this was no time for a nap. She stifled a yawn, started playing with her fingers, and stopped when she realised she was doing that.

Sankar continued. 'Despite what Bates had told Jonas, the British did not have plans to return the painting once they got their hands on it. This is what Bates told Samir.'

'What were they to do with it?'

'I really have no idea. Maybe the influential person wanted it in his or her private collection.'

'Oh.'

'So, after some four months, Jonas met Bates and told him that the work was complete and they were ready to replace the original painting with the fake. When Bates asked him how he could identify which was the original, Jonas pointed at the tree on the right in the picture. It had five leaves prominently painted in a straight line. All the leaves were roughly the same size. Herr Bormann said, "The fake has two of these leaves painted significantly smaller".'

'And he handed over the original to Bates?'

'I think they went to the place where the paintings were stored to protect them from air strikes and Jonas did the replacing, but I am not really sure of the details there. But yes, he apparently handed over the original to Bates after doing the switch. At least that was what he thought. He collected the painting and went straight to London. However, he had to leave for another assignment in India shortly afterwards. By the time he reached India, the British government had sent information to Kolkata that the painting Bates had handed over in London was a fake. And that was why the officer came to see the sick Bates time and again.'

'What?'

'The salt mine where the paintings were stored were heavily affected by the fire; many artworks were lost and Jonas was dead. So, there was no way to pursue that lead.'

'How did they know it was a fake? Did they conduct tests on the painting?'

'No, it was right in front of their eyes. They just took a little time to realise it.'

'Let me guess. Bates had replaced the original with another fake before handing it over to Number 10?'

'Bates did no such thing. Jonas had had at least two copies of the painting made and double-crossed the British government that had originally planned to con him. He had lied to Bates about the leaves. It is the original where the leaves are of different sizes,' the doctor said. 'Bates died in the early hours the following day.'

After the young woman had left, the doctor came back from the door and sat down on his favourite couch. His wife sat on the one facing him.

'You were hoping she'd say it,' she said.

'I was praying for her to say it! I read every line of that letter, looking for the clue that she might have missed. But it looked to me a lover's note…After so many years—wow! You will have to agree this is thrilling, Ivy,' Sankar said.

'It is! But Sankar, what are the chances that she might have told you the phrase and you'd missed it?'

'It is supposed to be a simple and self-evident phrase, based on the information I already have. And the person saying it will have read it in a letter. From what I understand, I will know it when I hear it.'

'I have a feeling we shall see that girl again,' Ivy said and smiled.

'Considering it is a story that has been passed on from grandfather to father to him, Sankar knew way too many specifics,' she told herself as she cleared security at Netaji Subhas Chandra Bose International Airport that evening.

2012

THE ONE REGRET

Art dealer Harold James Pemberton had no desire to celebrate his fifty-fifth birthday. He thought he was way too old and way too busy to waste time on such useless rituals. His 46-year-old girlfriend thought otherwise. Judy had insisted that they at least dine out. She chose Chutney Mary, one of London's most upscale restaurants, for dinner. At 7.45 pm sharp, they were seated at the table.

Harold wasn't really what one would refer to as a foodie, but when he sank his teeth into the Hyderabadi lamb *shank dum*, he turned to Judy, smiled, and said, 'Thank you.'

Judy leaned forward and kissed him on the cheek. Then she wiped off with her napkin a bit of gravy she had planted on Harold's cheek along with the kiss.

The two were yet to move in together, but over the past couple of days, Harold had seriously been considering it. Judy surprised him with small things when he least expected it and he loved her for it.

They left the restaurant at 9 pm. Harold dropped Judy at her apartment and decided to give his old man a visit on the way home.

Richard George Pemberton usually went to bed by 10 pm. But today was special. It's not every day that his son found time to see him. Harold adored and looked up to him. So, when the call from Harold came at 9.40, he made sure he did not fall asleep. At 92, that is tougher than you would imagine.

Only three people had free access to Richard's huge bedroom-cum-study. Apart from the father and the son, the third person was Richard's butler, Frank, who had been working at the Pemberton household for 34 years now.

As he entered the room, Harold let his eyes linger on the masterpieces that adorned the walls. Most of the world was not even aware that some of those paintings still existed. 'I will never get used to it,' he said to himself as he stared for a few seconds at Raphael's *Portrait of a Young Man*, which hung behind Richard's head and was regarded by many as the most important painting to have gone missing since the Second World War.

Lying in his bed, Richard looked at his son. 'You could have come a little early.'

'Sorry, Father. I hate to disturb you at this time, but I just felt like seeing you on my birthday.'

'Oh, it's your birthday, is it? I am sorry, it had totally escaped my mind. Well, happy birthday, son. I hope you enjoyed your day.'

'Doesn't matter. I don't like to celebrate, anyway. Tell me how you are doing. Dr Atkins tells me you've not been taking your medicines regularly.'

'Do you know how many pills I take every day, Harold?'

'No. How many?'

'14 on a good day.'

'Oh, that's a lot.'

'Son, I am 92. I think I have lived my life fairly well and on my terms. I have achieved and got most of the things I wanted to. It troubles me to think I now need to take at least 14 pills to take me through a single day. Old age is a bitch.'

'Everyone gets there, Father. That's no reason for you to not take your pills. And every time I enter this room and see all these priceless pieces of art, I know this is what you've wanted and this is what you achieved for yourself. You shouldn't complain about your life.'

'You of all people know the lengths to which I have gone to get hold of these. I have not been a particularly nice and honest person.'

'Nice and honest people die with regrets. You will not.'

The old man laughed with some difficulty. 'Is that what you think, son? That I do not have any regrets?'

'You do? Is there something you wanted to achieve but couldn't?'

'Yes. Oh yes.'

'Do you want to tell me about it?'

'Could you hand me that glass of water, please?'

Harold took the glass to his father and helped him drink a few sips. 'What were you saying about your regrets?'

'Not regrets. Just the one.'

'And that would be?'

'You see the painting behind me?'

'The Raphael?'

'Yes. You know how much I love it, don't you?'

'Probably more than me and Mother put together.'

Richard laughed his throaty laugh again. Too much laughing tired him out. He waited for a while before speaking. 'Your mother must be turning in her grave! But yes, I love that painting more than most things I have come across in my life. But had I managed to get my hands on this other painting, the Raphael would be hanging somewhere else in the room.'

'What painting was that?'

'It was a Van Gogh. That man knew how to use colours. I had seen it but once. It was the most fascinating sight of my life. You'd understand if you saw it. A man in a hat walking down a road in a Mediterranean summer with a canvas and a few other things. I don't know what it was about the painting, but I could just look at it for hours at a stretch and not get bored.' Speaking so much at a time was tiring for Richard. He stopped talking and stared ahead.

'You are not talking about *The Painter on his Way to Work*, are you?'

'Also known as *The Painter on the Road to Tarascon*. Yes, I am.'

'Holy crap! What happened?'

'I even had Uncle Winnie on my case. But it didn't work out. God, I loved that painting.'

'Are you serious? Is it still around?'

'He was interested in art, though hardly any good at painting himself. When the bloody Nazis were destroying art left and right, I had convinced the prime minister to conduct a secret mission to recover this one painting from Magdeburg in Germany. But the field agent's contact double-crossed him and gave him a fake.'

'Why didn't we grill the contact?'

'Both he and the guy who painted the fake were dead before we realised it was not the original. It was probably the best copy of any work that I'd seen. And I've seen quite a few of them in my time. You can say the Raphael was kind of my consolation prize.'

'How come you never told me about this before?'

'Never came up, I guess. And I'd rather not dwell on my failures.'

'So, you are saying the original could be hanging on some wall like this Raphael.'

'That is possible.'

'Are you too tired to talk for a few minutes now, Father?'

'I think I can stay awake for a bit. Why?'

Harold made himself a drink and returned to the chair next to Richard's bed. 'Tell me everything I need to know about the Van Gogh. I'll give it a try.'

'People are supposed to give you presents on your birthday, Harold. Not the other way round.'

'Then let me start the reverse trend,' he smiled. 'I love you, Dad.'

At 8.40 am, Patel put a hand out from under his blanket and felt around the bedside table till he found his phone. He glanced at the screen.

My office at 9. The text message had come at 6.45 am.

'Crap.' He jumped out of bed.

The man sat on the toilet with a toothbrush in his mouth at 8.41 am. When he left the apartment seven minutes later, no one seeing the 43-year-old Indian-origin man in a smart grey jacket would imagine he had seen Harold's message only eight minutes ago.

Ratnesh Patel did Harold's dirty work. He was resourceful and efficient and Harold paid him well. It was the perfect business relationship.

He entered Harold's office at 9.01 am.

'This is a first,' said Harold, looking at the clock over the door. 'You being late, even if it's just by a minute.'

'Sorry, Mr Pemberton. I overslept.'

'Sit down, Patel. We have work to do.'

Over the next hour, Harold explained to Patel how he wanted him to go about this operation. Patel frequently interrupted him to ask questions and took notes.

By 10 am, they had made two phone calls and set the plan in motion.

2012

WORK TRIP TO GERMANY

Eva certainly wasn't as much into me as I was into her. Though we'd had some chats on the phone after she left and I told her I'd broken up with Tina, it was mostly one-sided and the chemistry appeared to have fizzled out. It seemed that the out-of-sight-out-of-mind thing had set in.

I accepted the fact that now I had neither a girlfriend nor the girl I was insanely interested in. I immersed myself in work over the next few months. In the first week of April, Shreya told me we had an invitation from the German National Tourism Board to do a couple of stories in Berlin and she wanted me to go.

'It's a four-day trip, and if you want, you can extend it by a few more days and go see a few other places in the country too,' she added.

'Thanks, Shreya!'

'You sound a little too enthusiastic.'

'It's about a cute girl with cuter dimples,' I grinned and began writing an email to Eva.

There's this thing about writing emails and messages to people you're interested in. I write and edit stuff for a living. But when it comes to girls I have liked over the years, I have no idea why expressing the simplest things had turned out the hardest to put into words. It was no different this time around. After thinking for hours, among other things of whether I should use 'will be visiting' or 'will be going', the draft finally came out like this:

Dear Eva,

I will be visiting Berlin for work for a few days at the beginning of April.

It would be fun if we could catch up. We could go to Tempelhof Airport and have a picnic or just sit and chat maybe? Or maybe catch a German movie together. You know, I've actually watched a German movie in the theatre! It was a Swiss-German one, which of course is somewhat different from German. I know I wouldn't understand any of it, but it will be fun, don't you think? I know you love gelato. Maybe you could take me to your favourite gelato place? It'll be my treat, of course!

But I don't want to have you bored going around Berlin too much, because it's your city. So, I was thinking we could do a short trip—say two days—and go out of the city? What do you think?

Best,
Neil

The call came at 10.15 am, when Harold was in his office. He asked his secretary to leave the room and took it. 'What have you got for me?'

'We've managed to trace the families,' said Patel.

'Good. Give me the details.'

'Five years after Jonas Bormann died, Claudia got married to Marco Schicktanz. In 1952, they had a son called Mathias. This son got married to Andrea in the early 1980s. They had a daughter, who was born in 1984.'

'What else?'

'When the Hungary border opened in 1989, Mathias and Andrea moved to Wuppertal in West Germany with their daughter, where the family has been living ever since.'

'What about Claudia and Marco?'

'They stayed back in Magdeburg, but I am not sure why.'

'Maybe they decided they were too old to move?'

'That could be a reason,' said Patel. 'But we don't know for sure yet. Marco died in 1998. In 2000, Claudia moved to a seniors' home. She recently passed away.'

'How recently?'

'Just a couple of weeks ago.'

'Tell me about Mathias and his family,' said Harold.

'The couple runs a small café in Wuppertal that is popular with the local university students. The daughter is a university student in Berlin. She is not in Wuppertal at the moment, but I'm not sure if she's in Berlin either.'

'Did you look up the other family?'

'Yes. Alois Bischof, who was known as Al, did not marry or have kids. His father died somewhere in the early forties and we know Al died in 1945. His mother moved in with a sister of hers some time after Al's death. She died in the late sixties or early seventies. No surviving direct family there.'

'Good job, Patel.'

'Thank you, Mr Pemberton.'

'Now find out where the girl is.'

'I will do that,' said Patel and disconnected the call.

Harold clicked open a file on his desktop. The picture filled the monitor. He stared at it for a full two minutes.

'I think I know what Father meant when he said he could stare at it for hours and not get bored,' he whispered to himself.

2012

AN ACCIDENTAL MEETING

'Hallo, Mama.'

'Hallo! You need to go to Magdeburg once again.'

'What do I have to do there?'

'A lawyer called. He said your grandmother left you something in a will.'

'I wonder what that could be. But don't you guys have to come too?'

'No, it's just for you. That's what the man said. Go over sometime next week when you find time. Now note down the address,' she said, and dictated as the young woman jotted it down on a writing pad.

'I am really curious now. I will go as early as I can.'

Hi Neil,

It was good to get your email saying you will be in Berlin. Unfortunately, there's a big chance I will not be in the city around that time. But do let me know when you are here and I will try to catch up.

Hugs,

Eva

'Hugs'. Yes, that was the word I should have used. 'Best' was so formal! Why didn't the perfect words come to my mind when they were needed?

Eva's email did not dampen my sprits much, and I still had hope that something would work out and we would be able to meet. But when I sent her a message the moment I landed in Berlin, she replied saying sorry because she would not be here.

I finally resigned myself to my fate and immersed myself in the job at hand.

This was my fifth visit to Berlin, my second-most favourite city after Kolkata. If asked to choose between Berlin and Paris, a lot of people I knew would instantly have said Paris. I, on the other hand, would have chosen Berlin without a second thought. This energetic and complicated city with its historical baggage, too many tourists, awesome parties and currywürsts made me fall in love with it every time I was there. On top of that, the city was among Europe's cheapest capitals.

'*Berlin ist arm, aber sexy*,' the city's mayor Klaus Wowereit had famously said in a television interview in 2004. *Berlin is poor, but sexy*. I couldn't have agreed more.

As part of the assignment, I went around the city visiting its various landmarks over three days. But that was certainly not all I was doing, because by the end of my official trip, I had already filed three stories.

'Very efficient!' Shreya messaged me. 'Now take a break.'

Yes, now was the time for a little holiday. I had been reading some Second World War history ahead of this trip, and wanted to visit a place that had been affected by the war and that which I hadn't visited before—one which hordes of tourists hadn't discovered yet. I could possibly have gotten ideas for some stories while I was there, too.

Magdeburg seemed like the perfect place. It is not too far from Berlin and certainly not a touristy city. Everyone in Berlin who I spoke to about the place said it would be quite a boring place to visit, especially after spending time in the energetic capital.

I took a morning intercity express train and reached the town in one hour and 40 minutes. The city by the river Elbe had been completely flattened during the Second World War by the British air force and so, just like Hiroshima, I was happy to see that it had been rebuilt wonderfully.

I switched on the map on my phone and realised my guest house wasn't too far from the station, and so I decided to walk. Once outside the station, I took what looked like a little shortcut through some buildings and reached Otto-von-Guerickestraße, a busy road on which trams ran, apart from regular vehicles. I crossed it and walked right along it till I reached the Kulturhistorisches Museum, which I intended to see during this visit. I took the left just before the museum—Danzstraße—and walked straight for a few minutes to reach Breiter Weg. Across the road I could see the Magdeburg Cathedral, locally known as Magdeburger Dom, the city's best-known landmark.

My guest house was in an alley just a couple of hundred metres away and I checked in, kept my bags in the room and went out again to find a nice place for lunch. I planned to spend a couple of days there.

I entered what looked like a cozy place by Breiter Weg and found a seat by the window. I was enjoying some delicious gnocchi and updating my travel journal when I saw her briskly walking down the pavement on the other side of the main road.

The secretary asked her to wait and she sat on the dark blue sofa playing with her fingers. After 10 minutes, she called the visitor and showed her into the office of the lawyer.

The lawyer was professional and did not believe in small talk. He directed her to one of the two chairs facing him across his desk and asked for her ID. After looking at it closely, he said, 'Everything seems to be in order. Please wait for a minute.'

She smiled and nodded.

He went into a room attached to his office and came back with the box that she had gone through several weeks ago, when she had last met her grandmother.

'Do you recognise this box?'

'Yes,' she said. 'I saw it in my grandmother's room when I last met her.'

'Here you go. Your grandmother had asked me to give it to you,' he said and handed it over.

'Thank you,' she said, picking up the photograph of a young Claudia from inside the box.

'There is one more thing.'

She looked up and he handed over an envelope that had 'Claudia' written on it. It reminded her of the letter she already had. This one looked just as old as the other one. But since she had reread the other letter many times, she knew from a glance at this one that they had not been written by the same person.

'Thank you,' she said once more and placed it in her pocket. Then she lifted the box and proceeded to walk back to her hotel that was five blocks away. The call came as soon as she closed the door of her room.

'Hallo, Neil!'

'Eva, why are two men following you?'

Patel swiped the green receive button on his phone screen. 'Tell me.'

'She collected a medium-sized cardboard box from the lawyer's and went back to her room. What do we do?'

'Wait for the right moment and do a clean job,' he said and disconnected the call.

2012

BOX OF MEMORIES

'Where are you now? Can you still see them?' Eva asked me.

'No, I lost you guys around a corner. Which one is your hotel?'

After she told me the name, it took me five minutes to find it. But the two men were nowhere to be seen. I told Eva so.

'Is there a chance you might have been mistaken?'

'I guess I could have been...'

'Hold on. It's a nice day outside. Why don't you wait for me at the cafe with the blue chairs across the street from my hotel? I'll join you in 10 minutes.'

I had only eaten half my gnocchi before rushing out of the other restaurant and ordering a quiche and coffee. Eva joined me soon after. She wore a cream-coloured pullover on a white T-shirt along with dark blue jeans and sneakers. She carried a sling bag. We hugged.

'It's good to see you, Eva.'

'I'm glad I could meet you, too. Actually I had to go visit my parents in Wuppertal and then come here to collect something my grandmother has left me. She died a couple of weeks ago. That's why I couldn't be in Berlin the last few days. You're leaving day after tomorrow, right?'

'Yes,' I said.

'Actually, I was thinking of returning to Berlin tomorrow evening and surprising you. But you found me before that,' she said and grinned.

'Was the stuff you were carrying the things your grandma left you?'

'Yeah. Just some memories.'

'I still kind of have the feeling I saw the two men following you, all right,' I said, and turned my gaze to Eva's hotel to see what I thought were the same men leaving. One of them had a big sling bag on him. 'That's them leaving your hotel,' I said and jumped up.

Eva turned to see the last man disappear behind the next building.

'Do you have something important or valuable in your room, Eva?'

'Yes, you could say that,' she replied.

I fished out a €10 and a €5 from my wallet and kept them on the table. 'Let's go check on them.'

We rushed across the street and into the hotel, didn't wait for the elevator but ran up the stairs to the second floor. Eva opened the door. It opened into a narrow corridor that had a toilet to the right. There was a room with a single bed, a small table and a window on the wall opposite to the door overlooking the street. I could see Eva's bag on the floor, and some clothes and underwear strewn on the bed. The box was on the table.

'It's empty,' said Eva, looking inside it.

'I saw one of them with a sling bag.'

'And my two letters are missing too.'

'Were the letters in the box as well?'

'I had left them by the box on the table here.'

'Why would people want to steal some memories that your grandmother left you?' I wondered aloud.

'Because it was much more than just memories.'

'Excuse me?'

'I'll tell you about it.'

'Shouldn't we complain to the hotel authorities about this?'

'No. Now that they have it already, that will not help much. And I have copies of the letters.'

'I am totally lost here. If you're going to tell me what's going on, please do so now.'

Eva took out her phone and opened an image. 'Zoom and read,' she said and handed it over to me.

It was a letter. Yellow and worn.

My dear Claudia,

You must be wondering why I am writing to you in English. Well, I just want to check if you have learnt the language well enough or not!

Do I see you smile? I am glad for that, my dear, because if you are reading this letter, I am probably dead and I don't want you to brood over it. The war is about to end and you are young. I would like nothing better than you starting things anew. I wish you all the best.

I just have one request. Never lose this letter, because I am writing to you four important words here—'FROM ARLES TO CALCUTTA'.

This is a powerful phrase if used at the right place. But whom it should be told to, I hope you will be able to figure out, my darling.

Your loving husband,

Jonas
Magdeburg
28 April 1945

'What is this about?'

'Long story. And that's one of the letters. Jonas was the first husband of my grandmother.'

'Long story later. Let's just get those buggers off our tail and sit and think this out.'

In an hour or so, we both checked out of our hotels. Then we walked together to the central station. We reached there around 4 pm and took the next train out of town.

'Neil, do you think they are still following us?'

'Yes. I saw one of the guys get on the same train.'

'What now?'

'Just sit and wait. There is no use running on the train.'

In five minutes, the man walked into the compartment from behind and sat when he found an empty seat three rows in front of us.

When the train stopped at Halle, he turned back to see if we were still in our seats. As soon as he turned his back on us again, we grabbed our bags and ran to the doors. They closed as soon as we jumped out and he was there five seconds later, frantically pushing the button to open the doors as the train pulled out.

'That was good, Mr Bond,' Eva grinned. 'Now what?'

'Let's go to Berlin.'

We took the 17.48 intercity express to Berlin. Once seated, I asked quietly, 'Do you now want to fill me in on what's happening?'

Eva pushed her glasses up her nose and said, 'Like I told you, it's a long story. And Neil, I hope you understand how important it is to keep what I am going to tell you to yourself.'

'Of course. There are goons following us and we have an hour and 13 minutes to kill on this train.'

'So here's the story. My grandmother used to stay in Magdeburg, and last year, I had gone to see her. She was well over 90 at that point. We had a little chat and that's when I discovered the other letter that you have not seen yet.'

'What does that one say?'

'It's basically a love note. My grandmother had an affair with this British guy she had met during the last months of the war. I did not find anything unusual with the letter—until she told me that Herr Bormann, her first husband, who was the curator of the Kaiser-Friedrich Museum, and this British guy, who was apparently a spy, were trying to save a painting. That's when I read the letter again and it struck me as a bit odd.'

'The Nazis were destroying a lot of art. But in what way was the letter odd?'

'The letter had a little too much information about the doctor who was treating Bates in Kolkata, considering it was the love note of a dying man. I wanted to ask Grandma more on this, but by that time she had fallen really ill and could not talk at all. Grandma was already senile when she told me about her lover, and though it was a long shot, I decided to go to Kolkata and try to find this doctor's family.'

'That's why you came to Kolkata?'

'Yes. I tried, but couldn't find them that time.'

'When did you do that?'

'It was on the evening of the second day of our stay when you went to see your parents. So, the next day, I approached a private detective agency to do this for me.'

'Did that work?'

'They called me right after you left Delhi. The family had sold their North Kolkata property, the address of which was mentioned in the letter, and moved to the southern part of the city. I called them up right then and requested to meet. The grandson of Bates' doctor agreed to see me. I flew down soon after.'

'You came to Kolkata again!'

'Yes,' said Eva and smiled. 'The family was very helpful and friendly. The grandson, who is also a doctor, told me everything he knew about Bates. And he knew quite a bit! A little too much, I thought.'

'A little too much?'

'Considering this was a story that had been passed on from grandfather to father to him, he knew too many specific details,' said Eva.

'But what did you find out?'

'He said Herr Bormann had double-crossed the British by handing them over a copy of the painting instead of the original. Bates didn't realise it and gave that to the guys in London, who realised it was a fake only after a while. By that time Bates was in Kolkata. So, the situation now is that no one really knows where the real painting is at this point.'

'You mind telling me what painting it was?'

'It was a Van Gogh.'

'Don't tell me you're talking about *The Painter on the Road to Tarascon* that was destroyed in a fire?'

'You know more history than I'd imagined,' Eva smiled. 'It would cause quite a furore if it surfaced today, wouldn't it?'

'You bet it would! It is one of the most important paintings to have been lost in the Second World War,' I said. 'And I am not really an expert in World War history. I just had been reading up on Berlin and its nearby towns during the war before coming to Europe this time and that was one of the reasons I decided to visit Magdeburg. That's how I know about this painting.'

'My grandmother died a couple of weeks ago and the family was here for the funeral. I had so many things to ask her...But this lawyer had called my mother some days ago and said Grandma had left some stuff for me. That's why I had gone to Magdeburg this time.'

'Whoever is after the painting now has everything you needed to figure out what you now know,' I said. 'This is not good.'

'But what we have is a big head start. And he doesn't know where the doctor's family lives now. For that, he either needs to go to Kolkata or hire someone there to find out.'

'Don't you think you should talk to the doctor and update him on what's happening?'

‘From what he’s told me, he doesn’t really know anything that will help uncover the painting,’ said Eva and looked out of the window. ‘We’re about to reach Berlin.’

‘Let’s not go to your apartment. That’s the first place they’ll check in Berlin. Let’s get into a guest house, get some rest and figure out things.’

‘Good idea,’ said Eva and squeezed my hand.

2012

THE KOLKATA CONNECTION

'Six photographs, two German books. This looks like a tiara, a brown scarf and a silver ring. That's all we have here. And apart from those in the box, she had these two letters,' said the man.

'Thanks. You can leave now,' said Patel.

After the door closed, he dialled Harold's number. 'Would you be able to find some time to meet me this morning, Mr Pemberton?'

Patel never requested a meeting at such short notice unless it was important. 'You can come over right now,' he said.

In 20 minutes, the two of them were locked up in Harold's office, poring over the items.

'What ought to be our next move?' said Harold.

'I am not sure. It would have been difficult to smuggle paintings out of Germany during the war. But this Bates guy was a spy and well connected. So, it is a little difficult to figure out what was going through his mind. If I were him, I would probably have hidden it well somewhere in Magdeburg itself and waited for the war to end,' said Patel.

'You have noticed the phrase Herr Bormann wrote in his letter to Claudia, haven't you?' said Harold.

'"From Arles to Calcutta". Yes, I did.'

'Does that not indicate the painting went to, or is still, in Kolkata? In case you are not aware, Van Gogh completed this painting in Arles,' said the art dealer.

'You are possibly right. But somehow it still strikes me as implausible. Couldn't he just keep it in England?'

'Yes, but I have this feeling that it was not Bormann who had double-crossed Bates, but the spy himself who conned us. They were possibly working together.'

'You mean he kept the painting with himself all along and took it to Kolkata with him? In that case, he would need access to a second fake,' said Patel.

'You have a point, but it is possible that Bates and Herr Bormann had had two fakes made. One for swapping the original and one as a backup.'

'And when replacing the original went smoothly, Bates took the second fake...Maybe he told Herr Bormann he'd destroy it. That is a plausible theory,' Patel said. 'But does that mean you are totally discarding the theory that the two of them could have been working together the whole time?'

'I don't know. The phrase hints otherwise. The Kolkata connection feels way too strong here,' said Harold.

'So, what would you like me to do now, Mr Pemberton?'

'I will sleep on this and see if I come up with anything. I am almost sure we have everything the girl had to figure things out by herself, which I assume she has, at least partially. At your end, you keep a watch on her. She has been to India, and I am sure she's paid a visit to Kolkata too. It is likely she went to India just to visit Kolkata. At this point, I am not even sure she got one or both the letters from the lawyer along with the box, or if she had got them from Claudia much before that.'

'The girl and her Indian friend gave us the slip, sir. I am sorry. We are trying our best to trace them as soon as possible,' said Patel.

'Fire your inept men and hire able ones, Patel. I pay you well because I prefer working with professionals. Find her as soon as possible and please be discreet this time. And get someone else to tail her,' said Harold icily.

'Yes, Mr Pemberton.'

'Station a guy outside her Berlin apartment. She will go back sooner or later,' said Harold. 'And if by any chance you find her applying for a visa to visit India, you and I are going to India too.'

2012

SOME MORE THEORIES

'Where on Earth is Arles?' I asked.

We had found a guest house in a quiet part of Neukölln and moved into a comfortable room that had two single beds. We had picked up a döner kebab and some beer from a local joint for dinner, which we had in our room after freshening up.

'It's the place in southern France where Van Gogh had painted this particular painting,' Eva said as she slipped into her blanket. 'And you are pronouncing it wrong. It's like "Earl" but with an "A". And you have to pronounce the "R".'

'A-R-L-E-S. And the "S" is silent,' I said.

'I guess it's just the way the French people say things,' said Eva.

'Enough with the stupid pronunciation,' I giggled. 'But then, this could be the big clue! That certainly indicates the painting went to Kolkata, right?'

At that precise moment it struck me that this was the first time the two of us were going to sleep in the same room, albeit in two different beds. We'll get there, I told myself, and again chided myself in my mind for thinking sexually about her. But then I didn't know why I should be angry about myself about getting interested in Eva. She didn't have her glasses on and I decided I even loved the few freckles dotting her cheeks.

'Probably. But I wish Herr Bormann hadn't been so direct. The bad guys will take no time to figure it out too,' said Eva and woke me out of my reverie.

'I'm sure there was some purpose behind it. Kolkata is a big city and finding a painting there just like that will not be a cakewalk,' I assured her. 'So, what now? Who could be this appropriate person to say the phrase to? After so many years, the person might be dead and gone.'

'If I remember correctly, the letter said "if used at the right place", not a person. Do you think that is significant? Or is that just another way of saying that the right person will be present at the right place and it should be told to him or her?'

'But the next sentence said "But who it should be told to", didn't it? So I think the first sentence is just talking about the circumstances, not a place in the literal sense. Let me have a look at the letter again,' I said.

'Bet this will confuse the bad guys too,' Eva laughed and handed me her phone.

I went through Herr Bormann's letter and also the photograph of a letter the English spy called Edward Bates had sent Eva's grandmother.

'So this place could be Kolkata too.'

'The only person I know who is connected to the painting in some way in Kolkata is Sankar, the doctor I spoke to. And I spoke to him for quite some time that day. If he knew anything about this, I am sure he would have told me. He told me everything in such great detail. It just seems implausible that he would not tell me if he knew. I am positive that he believed everything I said and that is why he shared so much with me. And from what I know, there is absolutely no chance of Herr Bormann knowing Samir, the doctor who treated Bates, because the curator was dead way before Bates even got to India.'

'We're kind of stuck on this road. So, the other big question—who the hell sent those two jokers to your hotel room in Magdeburg?'

'I can't think of anyone.'

'It was the British government that had deployed Bates to get the painting out, correct?'

'Err... Yes.'

'I can't believe those two worked for the British government if it has, in fact, decided to pursue the painting after all those years.'

'That's not what he told me. What Sankar told me was that the order had come from the prime minister's office at 10 Downing Street. But that did not necessarily mean it was Churchill's idea. It could have been someone close to the prime minister, someone close enough or influential enough to convince him to commission that mission,' said Eva.

'That complicates things,' I said. 'This means it could be the same guys who were after the painting in the first place. And we have no idea who they were.'

'But wouldn't they be really old now? I cannot believe such an old man masterminding this whole operation.'

'Maybe the mastermind is just like you,' I said.

'Just like me? What do you mean?'

'I mean maybe they're family of the original mastermind—son or grandson or something like that.'

'That's a likely theory.'

'Let's get some sleep now. It's been a long day. We'll figure things out tomorrow.'

'Yes, I guess I am somewhat sleepy. Sorry, I forget, when is it that you go back to India?'

'Day after tomorrow.'

'I wish you could stay till we sorted this out. You're basically the only person who knows the entire story apart from me.'

'A lot can happen in one day, Eva,' I said, and hoped it would, and I was not just thinking about the painting.

2012

FROM ARLES TO CALCUTTA

'Are you taking your pills?'

'Can we talk about more interesting things, son?' the old man said as he drank some juice. 'It's been a while since we had breakfast together. Let's enjoy our family time.'

Harold said, 'I wanted to tell you that we have made some progress on the Van Gogh front.'

'Ah yes, the present you promised me on your birthday! Do you know where it is?'

'I am not certain, but Kolkata seems like a possible place.'

'Kolkata! Is that not where the spy went after Berlin… and died?'

'Yes, Father. The curator of the museum appears to have left a clue—it's a phrase that needs to be uttered at the right place, or maybe a person. We're not sure which.'

'What is this phrase?'

'"From Arles to Calcutta".'

'And what happens when you say that at the right place or to the right person?'

'I have absolutely no idea. I suppose you find out when you say it. But I am guessing it could be pointing you to the right direction,' said Harold.

'And how do you deduce that? How are you sure it is a clue?'

'The man did the painting switch and wrote this in case he died any time soon. It sure seems like he did it so that someone would be able to find the painting. He hoped his wife would. But she was apparently too dumb to figure it out. And Arles! That's where Van Gogh painted it!'

Richard drank some more juice and said, 'In that case, maybe it is in Kolkata...sitting pretty on some wall now.'

'But where is this place where the phrase must be used? Are the people who're supposed to hear it even alive today?'

'They do not need to be alive, Harold. All they need is to pass on the information like I have done to you,' the old man said.

'Patel, apply for an Indian visa right away. I want you to go to Kolkata and find out about the living family of this Dr Samir Kumar Ghosh from the letter,' said Harold on the phone.

'What do you want me to do once I find them?'

'Use your judgement and tell an appropriate person this phrase.'

'Roger. I will apply for the visa today.'

'Also, find the bloody girl as soon as possible,' said Harold before ending the call.

'If you ask me, I think "the right place" is just misleading and of no significance. It's definitely about a person,' I said as Eva opened her eyes in the bed next to mine. I had been thinking about it most of the night...apart from Eva, sleeping a few feet away from me on a different bed.

'What?' She yawned.

'I'll tell you more when you wake up,' I said.

I was already sitting up on my bed. She turned towards me and sat up against the wall with the blanket covering her waist downwards. My gaze hovered on her thin nightdress. She was obviously not wearing a bra.

'Now that I am up, are you going to do nothing but stare at my boobs?' she said, rubbing her eyes.

'Sorry,' I mumbled. 'Could you please look the other way while I go to the toilet?'

She gave a knowing smile and turned towards the window. I slipped out of the blanket and dashed to the toilet with my morning wood on full display through my shorts. By the time I was out, Eva was dressed.

'Let's freshen up, go have breakfast somewhere close by and come back. I don't want to be out for a long time,' she said.

We were back in the room after an hour. Our room was rather small—two beds with a passage in the middle that ended at the wall on the east, which had a window on it. We sat on our beds again, facing each other.

'I think "the right place" is just misleading and is of no significance. It's definitely about a person, like the next sentence says,' I began.

'Could be. We really have hit a dead end, haven't we?'

'I have another theory. What about the person who painted the fakes? That wasn't Jonas Bormann, was it?'

'No, it was someone else,' Eva agreed.

'That person definitely knew something, didn't he?'

'But if that was the case, wouldn't Claudia be able to figure it out and tell him?'

'Only if she knew who the painter was. They were working secretly and I am not sure how much they had divulged to Claudia, maybe for her own safety,' I said.

'But Neil, here's my point,' said Eva. 'Why would Herr Bormann leave this message for Claudia if he thought she would not have access to the information needed to get in touch with the person to whom this phrase must be said?'

'You definitely have a point there…I have an idea. Since you said the doctor who you spoke to in Kolkata…what's his name?'

'Sankar.'

'Since you thought Sankar knew way too many details. Why don't you ask him if he knows about the painter as well? Then we can try to get in touch with that person's living family.'

When Patel found out that Eva hadn't returned to her apartment, he was worried. He had a hunch that even if Eva wasn't in Berlin by now, she would definitely be back within the next week or so. He deployed 15 men in the city to just walk around different neighbourhoods with many hostels and guest houses to see if they could possibly get a glimpse of the girl.

But Berlin sees 30 million tourists every year and there is no end of places to stay. So, this was a tall order for 15 people. But that didn't mean they would stop trying.

2012

THE RIGHT PERSON

'Hi, Sankar! This is Eva. Are you free to talk?'

'It's good to hear from you again. I am at the hospital, but I can spare a few minutes. Tell me.'

'I need some information and I called to ask if you could help.'

'I am listening.' Though he did not make it apparent, the doctor's heart started beating fast. *Is this it*?

'I need to know about the person who drew the fakes. Do you know anything about him or her?'

No, no, no. That's not what I'm looking to hear! 'Not that I can recall, but may I ask why you want to find out about this person?'

'I have something that I probably need to tell that person or his living descendants,' said Eva.

This is it. She doesn't know it, but this is it. 'I do not want to be too intruding, Eva, but would you mind telling me what this thing is that you want to tell them?'

'It's just something I read in a letter that my grandmother had received many years ago.'

'Is it some kind of a phrase?' The tension in the doctor's voice was apparent.

'Yes, but what's wrong, Sankar?' Eva said. 'How do you know it is a phrase? Do you know anything about this?'

'Tell me that phrase,' the doctor said.

Eva went quiet.

Sankar grew impatient. 'Eva, are you there? This is important. Tell me the phrase, please.'

'"From Arles to Calcutta",' Eva whispered.

Sankar checked the points one by one in his head. A simple and self-evident phrase, based on the information he already had—a phrase that the person who told him had read in a letter. This person was related to Herr Bormann. Even though Eva wasn't a blood relative, he knew this was it.

'Sankar...Are you still there?'

'Eva, it is time you booked a trip to Kolkata again.'

'What just happened?'

'Trust me. You are going in the right direction in your quest. I have been waiting far too long for someone to tell me that phrase.'

'Oh my gosh! It was you!'

'Technically, someone was supposed to say it to my grandfather. But under the circumstances, yes, I was the person you were supposed to say it to.'

'I have a thousand questions right now and I don't know where to start.'

'Then don't start! Just come over and we will talk face-to-face,' the doctor laughed and disconnected the call. He dialled Ivy to tell her that she had been right in thinking Eva was going to meet them again soon.

That evening, when I returned to the guest house with our takeaway dinner and some food for the next day's breakfast, Eva opened the door with a big smile.

'Tell me what happened,' I said.

She said, giggling and excited, 'Claudia was supposed to get in touch with Samir and tell him the phrase. That's the reason Bates had mentioned him in such detail in his letter. But she probably could not connect the dots, or it could also have been that she didn't have the courage to try to visit Kolkata to meet him.'

'Eva, cool down,' I laughed and high-fived her. I would have preferred a hug but was a little unsure, and making the first move was never my thing, anyway. But this was certainly a huge breakthrough.

But Eva hadn't finished and continued speaking. 'So right now, Sankar was the person to whom it was to be told! I'm going to Kolkata again,' she said, closed her eyes punched the air. Then she came forward and gave me a tight hug.

'I love you, Eva,' I wanted to say, but kept mum.

There was a moment of quiet after the cheerful celebration. I think Eva realised it too, but kept quiet. The hug lingered a little longer than a platonic one, and I kissed her neck. Ten seconds later, we still hadn't pulled apart and the only sound I could hear was her breathing. Eva responded with a kiss on my jaw. Moments later, we were devouring each other's faces and tearing off our clothes.

2012

BACK ON THE RADAR

I woke up first. A smile appeared on my lips as I noticed the blonde strands caressing the face inches away from mine. Eva opened her eyes right then and caught me looking at her.

'Good morning,' she mumbled.

'It sure is,' I grinned and kissed her.

'Go brush your teeth,' she laughed and pushed me away.

We took a long, hot shower together. To say I was sad would have been an understatement when, after an hour, we had to end it because I had a plane to catch. We fried some sausages and bacon I'd got the day before at the guest house kitchen and had them with bread and coffee at the adjoining dining space.

Then we came back to our room and she helped me with my packing. It was time to go.

I am not bad with goodbyes, but I knew this one was going to be tough. I hadn't told her in as many words, but

I knew she understood. And I knew she loved me too, for I had read in her eyes what her lips never said.

She walked me to the bus station. We held hands. I was to take a bus to Berlin Hauptbahnhof, from where I had a train to Frankfurt. My flight back home was from there.

We decided there wasn't much to fear at this point, since it was Eva who had told Sankar the phrase. She had informed Sankar about the theft at Magdeburg, and she needed to get the documents together for her visa application.

We kissed goodbye and looked forward to meeting in Kolkata soon.

Sankar went on the Internet and found out the phone number he needed the very night he received the call from Eva. It was a Sunday and it was quite late, and he decided to make the call the next day.

On Monday, the day Neil left for India from Germany, Sankar called the History of Art department at Oxford University. A woman picked up the phone after five rings.

'My name is Dr Sankar Ghosh, and I am calling from Kolkata. I would like to speak to the head of the History of Art department, please.'

'I am sorry, Doctor,' said the voice from the other end. 'But Professor Johnson is on leave. He will only be back next week. Would you like to speak to Professor Brown, who is in charge right now in the absence of Professor Johnson?'

'I'm afraid that will probably not serve my purpose. Would it be possible for you to give me Professor Johnson's mobile phone number?'

'Sorry, I am not authorised to do that. Why don't you call back next Monday?'

'I will do that,' said Sankar.

Ivy had been standing by her overexcited husband while he made the call. 'Is he not around?'

'He is on leave. Damn, I hate to wait now!'

'Don't get your blood pressure high in anticipation of Monday,' laughed Ivy. 'What's a thriller without a buildup to the climax?'

Eva returned to her Berlin apartment the day after Neil left. But Patel's men only saw her when she left home a couple of days later to pay a visit to the Indian visa office. Eva always liked to visit the visa office before she applied for a visa. That way, she could be sure all her documents were in order during the actual application. She got her documents together and went there three days after Neil left.

A man in a brown suit and striped white shirt who had been loitering in the area for the past several days pulled out his phone when he saw her and clicked open a picture.

'The girl is back on the radar,' said Patel on the phone.

'Good. Ensure she doesn't go off again,' said Harold.

'And she went to the Indian visa office this morning.'

'Just as I feared. She knows too much. Find out when she's going and book my tickets on the same flight. When are you leaving?'

'In three days.'

2012

A CALL FOR THE DEPARTMENT HEAD

No one gave Ratnesh Patel a second look when he appeared in the arrival area of Netaji Subhas Chandra International Airport in Kolkata. And why would they? He looked every bit an Indian, and unless you heard him speak English, you wouldn't be aware of the British accent. He spoke passable Hindi. Even that had the accent, but he only spoke when it was absolutely necessary.

He booked a cab and went to an upscale hotel on Sudder Street, the area in the city where backpackers preferred to stay because of the many budget hotels that were also available there.

Patel had chosen the area after some research. It was bang in the centre of the city. New Market, where you could get practically everything, was a five-minute walk away. The metro was less than 10 minutes away on foot. So, he could reach both the north and south of the city relatively quickly. He had decided to avoid taxis whenever possible because of the usually bad traffic conditions in the city, and preferred to take the metro.

He had reached the city in the afternoon and decided to rest that day. The next morning he walked to Park Street metro station and took a metro towards Dum Dum. Six stations later, he got down at Sovabazar. Then he used the GPS on his phone to find out Madan Mohan Tala Street. It was only a few minutes' walk northwards, and then he had to turn left.

Once he was there, he looked around for old people who looked like they lived in the area. Samir Kumar Ghosh had died 40 years ago and Patel was not sure whether he had lived here till the end.

He went ahead to a small shop that appeared to be selling everything from writing pads to soft drinks. The shopkeeper looked to be in his fifties.

'One Coke, please,' Patel said in Hindi.

'I don't have Coke. Do you want Thums Up or Pepsi?' the shopkeeper replied.

'Pepsi then.' Patel took his first sip and said, 'Are you from here?'

'Yes. I actually came here with my parents in the seventies.'

'Do you happen to know a doctor called Samir Kumar Ghosh who used to stay here?' asked Patel.

'I don't think I recall a doctor by that name,' the shopkeeper said after thinking for a minute. 'Does he not stay here anymore?'

'I'm talking about long back. He died in the seventies, I think. I am a historian based in Sweden and just trying to get in touch with the doctor's family.'

A girl in her teens came to buy bread. 'Rini, is your grandfather at home?' the shopkeeper asked her.

'He just came back from the market. Why?' she replied.

'Could you take this gentleman to him? He is a historian and looking for someone who used to live in this area. Maybe he can help.'

'You want to come now?' said the girl, looking at Patel.

Patel thanked them both, paid for his Pepsi and left with the girl. A two-minute walk brought them in front of an old three-storey building with long green windows. The girl opened the collapsible gate with keys she had with her and asked him to come in. On the left was a staircase going up and on the right was a room with some sofas and a centre table. The girl guided her into this room, switched on the ceiling fan, and asked him to wait while she found her grandfather.

The walls of the old house were definitely thick, because Patel could feel the difference in temperature right since he had entered the building. He made up a background story in his mind as he waited for the old man.

Ronen Mallick came downstairs after five minutes. The man, who seemed to be in his mid-seventies, wore a loose, light-brown kurta and pyjama bottoms. He had thick glasses and a Bengali newspaper rolled up in his right hand.

'Sorry to keep you waiting,' he said, entering the room. He placed the newspaper on the centre table and folded his hands in greeting.

'Namaskar. Please don't be sorry,' said Patel with a smile, as he stood up and folded his hands too. 'I am a complete stranger and your granddaughter, I suppose, brought me to your home...'

'Yes, Rini is my granddaughter. Tell me, how can I help you?' said Mallick, sitting down on the couch opposite Patel's.

Patel started with his story. 'Sir, my name is Anil Sharma and I have been living in Europe for most of my life. My parents had moved to the UK when I was a kid. Now I live in Stockholm. I am a historian and I am researching Indian doctors in pre-Independent India. During my research, I came across the name of Samir Kumar Ghosh, who used to stay in this area in the 1940s. So, I am just here to find out if it was possible to get in touch with his family.'

'That is interesting, and yes, I do know Samir Kumar Ghosh,' said Mallick.

'That is wonderful.' Patel hoped he didn't look too happy.

'Most people who are around my age would know the doctor, I suppose. The family moved to South Kolkata in the early 1970s. As far as I know, he passed away soon after.'

'Do you happen to know their current address?'

'I am afraid not. But I think I can find it out for you. I will give you my phone number. Please give me a call at six this evening. I will try to find out their address by then,' he said.

'Thank you so much,' Patel said, standing up.

'You're welcome, but don't go just yet. Please have a cup of tea before you leave,' said Mallick.

'I would love to, but I still have a few places to visit today,' said Patel, and wrote down Mallick's phone number.

When the professor returned to his office after teaching a class on Monday afternoon, his research assistant Penny said, 'Professor, a Dr Sankar Ghosh called you from Kolkata a little while ago. I asked him to call in half an hour. I think you can expect his call in the next 10 minutes.'

'I don't think I have heard that name before,' said Ryan Johnson as he sat down on his chair.

The phone rang after three minutes.

'That must be him, professor. Do you want to take it?'

'Yes, I will take it,' he said, picking up the phone. 'This is Ryan Johnson.'

'Professor Johnson. Good to be able to get in touch with you, finally. My name is Sankar Ghosh. I am a doctor based in Kolkata. I just want to confirm, you are the head of the History of Art department at Oxford University, right?'

'That is correct. But what is this about, doctor?

'I have something that I need to tell you.'

'Go ahead. I am all ears.'

'From Arles to Calcutta,' said Samir slowly. 'Does that mean anything to you?'

Johnson went quiet, and then he stood up. 'This is not a joke, right?'

Penny noticed. 'Is everything okay, professor?'

'It certainly is not a joke,' said the voice from the other side. 'As far as I knew, you were supposed to be expecting this call for a while now.'

Johnson took a while to take it in. Once he got himself together, he gestured to Penny that he was fine.

'Professor, are you with me?' Sankar said from the other side.

'After nearly 70 years! Are you kidding me? I never imagined you would actually call up, especially after all these years,' said Johnson.

‘So, it does mean something.’

‘It sure does. But I am not the person who you are supposed to talk to. I will give you his home number. He doesn’t use a mobile phone,’ said Johnson.

Then Johnson told Sankar the name and phone number of the person who had retired from the same department a decade ago.

2012

THE ONE MAN WHO KNEW

Ronald Gellar's association with Oxford's History of Art department had been long. He had earlier been a research scholar in the very department where he had taught for 33 years.

When he was working on his DPhil thesis on British architecture in Victorian Kolkata, Walter Bates was his guide. The two got on well together, and consequently Ronald was eager when he was offered a faculty position at the department.

His teaching career had been eventful, but when he thought about the most exciting moment of all his years at Oxford, one event came easily to his mind.

It was an evening in 1971, some three years after he had joined as a teacher, when Professor Bates had called him over to his office and closed the door.

'I have something important to share with you, Gellar. And you cannot talk to anyone about it. Can you promise me that?'

'Of course, Professor. What is this about?'

'You're young and I believe you will be here for a long time. I am going to retire in six months. So, I think you are the best person to share this secret with,' said Bates. He was not smiling.

'I am really curious now, Professor,' Gellar said.

'First, I cannot emphasise enough the importance of not sharing with anyone what I am about to tell you. At least, not until the time is right.'

'I understand.'

'Then listen carefully. For the past 26 years, the head of this department has been waiting for a call from Kolkata.'

'The head of department keeps changing. How does that work?'

'Everyone who is appointed head for the first time is told about this on their first day. Their job is basically to transfer the call to me.'

'But how do they know which call is the call you've been waiting for? And what's this all about?'

'The caller is supposed to say a particular phrase,' said Bates. 'And then they know the call is for me. But I am old. What if I'm not around to take that call when or if it comes? So, that responsibility will go to you. Please understand, Gellar, that this is a big responsibility of historical importance. I know, as a lover of art, this will get you excited, but you need to carry out your part when the time comes. Everyone else just knows that they have to transfer the call and nothing more. I am now going to tell you what it is really about.'

'Okay, Professor,' he said, staring blankly at Bates' face.

'First, you should know I had a brother called Edward. It is with him that the story begins. And second, the phrase is "From Arles to Calcutta". That is the exact phrase you are looking to hear,' Bates said and proceeded to explain what Gellar should do once the caller uttered those words.

After 30 minutes, Ronald Gellar left the professor's office shaking in excitement.

Walter Bates died in 1990. Ronald Gellar retired in 2002. No one really believed the call would come now.

Ronald was getting ready to go out and meet with some friends at a local bar when Sankar called. The two spoke for a few minutes. After disconnecting that call, Ronald dialled one of the friends he was supposed to be meeting that evening and said that he was sorry, because something had come up and he could not make it. He called up his son Nathan and asked him if he could come over right then. Then he walked up to his wife, who was reading a book curled up on the couch.

'Emma, Nathan is coming over for dinner. We have something to talk about,' he told his wife. 'I have some important things to say both to you and Nathan.'

Dinner got over quickly because Ronald decided not to interfere with everyone's enjoyment of Emma's wonderfully cooked medium-rare steak with vegetables and mashed potatoes. Once they were done, the three of them sat in the living room with drinks in their hands.

'This suspense is killing me, Dad. Can we start already?' Nathan said.

'I am sorry for taking my time, Nathan. But yes, let's get to it right now. Tonight, I am going to tell you a secret that I had been keeping within me for no less than 41 years,' Ronald said.

'Really?' Nathan was a little surprised.

'So, you're saying even I don't know this?' said Emma.

'No. I am sorry, my dear. The issue was such and I chose to tell no one at all.'

'So why do you want to tell us this secret now?' she asked, visibly a little irritated.

'Because the time has finally come when I think I can share it with the people closest to me on this planet.'

'I'm on the edge now. Spill it,' said Nathan. 'My exhibition is tomorrow and I would have liked to spend some more time getting things just right.'

'Another reason I have called you tonight is because you are an artist, Nathan, and I believe this will interest you. Among the most famous works of art to have been destroyed or lost during the Second World War is Van Gogh's *The Painter on the Road to Tarascon*, which used to be on display at the Kaiser-Friedrich Museum in Magdeburg. This museum, as you would know, has a new name now—Kulturhistorisches Museum.'

'I know that. What about it?' Nathan sounded just a little impatient.

'That painting was not destroyed.'

'What?'

'Yes,' said Ronald with a twinkle in his eye. 'The painting survived and today, I am the only person in the entire world who not only knows that the painting was not destroyed, but also where to look to find it.'

'What are you saying?' Nathan looked stunned.

Emma wasn't so much into paintings, but she realised the gravity of the situation from the tone of Ronald's voice and Nathan's reaction. She remained quiet and looked at Nathan as he spoke.

'What's special about today? Why did you call me today and not any other day?'

'I have much to find out myself, but from what I understand, a young German woman started a chain reaction that leads to the location of the lost painting. I am a link in that chain. The link before me gave me a call today from Kolkata. And you know what? We had been waiting for this call for 67 years!'

'But it's good it came late. Otherwise you wouldn't be part of the chain at all, would you, dear?' Emma finally smiled.

Ronald laughed. He never ceased to appreciate his wife's quick wit. He turned his gaze to Emma and said: 'That's true, my dear. But I am not satisfied to remain just a link in the chain. As a keeper of this secret for more than four decades and as someone interested in art history, I want to be present when the painting is discovered.'

'And I assume you want me to go with you?' said Nathan. 'Where is the painting?'

'I would have asked your mother to come along, but as you know, her sister's daughter is getting married two weeks from now, and she is really looking forward to that. So, it's going to be just you and me heading to Kolkata.'

'I was guessing it would be somewhere in Europe! I'll talk to a travel agent tomorrow and get our tickets and visas done at the earliest.'

The doorbell rang less than an hour after Sankar had made the call to Ronald Gellar. Ivy took it to find a bearded man in jeans and a collared blue T-shirt with a sling bag.

'Is Dr Ghosh in?' he said in impeccable English.

'Yes. Could I ask who you are?' said Ivy.

'My name is Anil Sharma. I am a historian based in Sweden at the moment. I am researching native Indian doctors in pre-Independent India. During my research I came across the name of Samir Kumar Ghosh. I understand that Dr Sankar Ghosh is his grandson. So, it would be great if I could speak to him. I promise I will not take more than 10 minutes,' said Patel.

'Please come in,' said Ivy and guided him to the drawing room where Sankar was reading.

Ivy introduced the two of them and left.

'How can I help you, Mr Sharma?' said Sankar.

Patel put his hand into his left jeans pocket, pulled out a handkerchief and wiped his forehead. The weather was hot and humid and the rains had not started yet. What Sankar did not notice was that he had also pulled out a small black gadget along with the handkerchief, which he deftly transferred to his other hand.

'Sorry, it's too hot,' smiled Patel. 'I had come across your grandfather's name during my research and some cryptic information.'

'Cryptic information? Of what kind?'

'Tell me, Dr Ghosh, does the phrase "From Arles to Calcutta" mean anything to you?'

Dr Ghosh's face betrayed surprise for two seconds, but that was enough for Patel to figure that the doctor was aware of the phrase. Sankar did not meet Patel's eyes when he said, 'No, no, no, no, no.'

During the time Sankar looked elsewhere, Patel stuck the small gadget in his right hand in a corner under the table in front of him.

Sankar composed himself in a while and said, 'But where did you come across this phrase?'

'It's not important, since you do not know about it. But thank you for your time,' said Patel and stood up. 'I'll be off now.'

Patel left the doctor's home, put his earphones on, and went to a nearby café. He ordered a cold coffee and a sandwich, took out a little writing pad and pen from his bag, and made himself comfortable.

The doctor called up Eva after Patel left. 'Eva, do you remember telling me that the things your grandmother left you along with the letters were stolen?'

Eva sensed the panic in Sankar's voice. 'Yes, of course. What's wrong, Sankar?'

'A gentleman, who looked Indian and claimed to be a researcher in Stockholm, came to my house a little while ago, told me the phrase and asked if it meant anything to me. He had a strong British accent.'

'Crap. What did you tell him?'

'No, of course. I don't think I sounded convincing enough, though. He caught me off guard.'

'I can't believe they have reached Kolkata! This is creeping me out now,' said Eva.

‘Cool down. Kolkata is our city and it’s not easy for a foreigner to get hold of a painting like that and take it outside again. Don’t worry. We will figure it out. You just be careful yourself and keep your eyes and ears open. You are leaving for India in two days, right?’

‘Yes.’

‘Be careful. I’ll see you soon.’ Sankar disconnected the call and dialled Ronald Gellar. ‘I called to tell you that there are others on the painting’s trail.’ He went on to tell Ronald the details of what had happened that evening. Afterwards, he said, ‘On Saturday, are you going straight to your hotel from the airport or do you want to come to my place first?’

‘I have asked the hotel to pick us up from the airport. I think I’ll go there first, freshen up and then give you a call to decide where we could meet.’

‘I will wait for your call in the evening,’ said Sankar and disconnected.

Patel finished scribbling on the pad as he listened to the conversation between Sankar and Eva, and then with Ronald. The doctor appeared to be walking back and forth as he spoke on the phone, because the quality of reception wavered in that pattern. But he thought he had heard the important bits. Though he already knew that the girl was coming to India in two days, the conversation had confirmed his strong suspicion about the doctor being aware of the phrase. He also knew now about a certain Professor Ronald Gellar, who was also coming to Kolkata on 2 June. Things were certainly heating up.

This was Patel's first time in Kolkata, but he had been to Delhi and Mumbai many times before this and had made quite a few connections in India's political and financial capitals. These connections were unlikely to forget him in a hurry because of the amount of business he had brought them. Every time he had left, they told him time and again to call up if he needed any kind of help.

Patel called up Ashfaq Ali in Delhi. The place Ali called home was a cramped room inside a shabby building behind Jama Masjid in the crowded Chawri Bazar of Old Delhi. He lived with his mother and ran all sorts of shady businesses from there. However, when he travelled, which he did frequently, he allowed himself the luxury of staying at fancy hotels. He, of course, always paid in cash.

Ali was happy to get Patel's call and promised him that the things he required would reach his hotel in Kolkata in three days. He knew that, when he was working with Patel, money was never a problem.

Satisfied with his conversation with Ali, Patel dialled Harold Pemberton's number to update him on the day's developments.

2012

A SWELTERING DAY

1 June was a sweltering day. The rains hadn't started yet and humidity made the day even more uncomfortable. Eva was wearing a loose white top and blue jeans. She had a dark green backpack on her back and a black knapsack that she wore over her chest. Blond tresses covered her right eye and my heart skipped a beat the moment I saw her using her forefinger to stick that bit of hair behind her right ear. She smiled when she saw me and my eyes automatically went to her dimples.

We drove out of the airport and headed towards the city. 'So, are you going to stay at the hotel?' I asked.

'Sankar said someone else would be joining us. This person is staying at the Grand Hotel and I could stay there as well.' She looked at me and I guess how I felt showed on my face. 'Aww, Neil, but I will stay with you, of course,' she laughed.

I grinned and asked, 'Where are those people coming from? And how many are there?'

'They are flying in from the UK. I think just one or two people. I'm not a hundred per cent sure though. I need to check with Sankar. But I'm so tired. I need a shower and some sleep,' Eva said and yawned.

'They could be watching us right at this moment, isn't it?' I said and looked at the rearview mirror.

'There is that chance. Let's just keep our eyes open,' she said.

We drove to my place in South Kolkata through the evening traffic and it took around one-and-a-half hours to get to the South City mall, which is next to where I lived. Eva dumped her luggage and spent a full 30 minutes in the shower. I offered her a beer when she came out. She refused and said she just needed some solid sleep now and asked if we could talk afterwards. I, of course, said yes.

For now, I was satisfied just to sit on my couch and watch her fall asleep.

Patel had gone to pick up Harold at the airport. Harold had been on the same flights as Eva—from Frankfurt to New Delhi and New Delhi to Kolkata—he had of course made sure that she did not notice him. While Eva met Neil and got into his car, Patel instructed his driver, '*Peecha karo.*' *Follow them*. And so the driver did.

Once they had seen Neil park the car and the two of them getting into the building, they had turned back and gone to Patel's hotel at Sudder Street.

'I have a tab on Sankar, at least when he is home, and he is in the thick of things. We could possibly bug Eva's friend's place. But I am not sure if the risk is worth it,' said Patel.

'I need some sleep,' said Harold, who was still getting used to the incredible June heat and humidity.

'No problem. You freshen up and sleep. I have booked a room for you at my hotel. We'll talk once you are up around dinnertime.'

Harold slept for three hours. He called Patel after he had gotten out of bed and taken a shower, and he came over to his room with two beer bottles.

'The doctor got home a little while ago. So, we should be able to hear some conversation if he talks to the girl now,' said Patel. This professor Gellar is coming tomorrow. But I am not sure what time he's arriving and what he looks like. I could only hear one side of the conversation. But it appeared to me he will go to his hotel first. I'm not sure how to track him.'

'Let's just concentrate on Sankar. The Gellar guy will get in touch with him.'

'Do we need to track the girl and the local guy?'

'It would be great if you can, but I think it will be easier and make more sense to just concentrate on Sankar. Let's just tail him 24x7.'

'Then we'll station ourselves near his place early in the morning. The thing is, his wife knows what's going on, so they could be discussing it in regular conversation. But they speak Bengali at home. Hindi and Bengali are similar and I can pick up a few words here and there, but that's it.'

'Pick up whatever you can. If you think you've heard some familiar words, write them down. We will get it translated,' said Harold. 'Could you get hold of a gun?'

'I have spoken to this guy. He is running a little behind schedule, but a Mauser and six bullets should reach me by tomorrow evening. I did not take the risk of some country-made rubbish, which is easier to procure. And I have got a couple of other things too that could come in handy,' said Patel and pulled out from a bag two scary-looking kitchen knives. 'A meat knife and a carving knife. These should work well in an emergency.'

Eva woke up at nine on a Friday night and called up Sankar, who told her that Ronald, a professor from the UK, and his artist son Nathan were arriving on Sunday night. They decided that it would be good to meet on Monday morning so that everyone could tell their part of the story and everyone had a complete picture of what had been happening.

The next two days passed in a blur, and Sankar's call came at 8.10 pm.

2012

AN INCONSPICUOUS MAN

The man wore an untucked brown checked shirt and black trousers. Someone with a sense of contemporary fashion would not have approved of the white sneakers he wore. But then, he was on the job and attire that stood out did not agree with his line of work. Ashfaq Ali had told him to be as inconspicuous as possible and Lakhan Singh had worked on his looks. His well-oiled, thin hair lay flat on his pate, and his cheap, brown-rimmed spectacles sat awkwardly on his short nose. Every few minutes, he had to push the spectacles up his nose to keep them from falling off.

The sun was just about to rise when Lakhan collected the package from Ashfaq, stuffed it in his sling bag, and got into a taxi that took him to Agra. A train ride would have been way more comfortable, but the risk was not worth it. Of course, flying was out of question.

After a tiring journey, on the fourth morning since he had left Delhi, Lakhan Singh entered Kolkata.

From the Babughat bus terminus, he took a yellow cab, and got down in front of the Indian Museum. He had been to Kolkata before, but never inside the museum, where he had heard that, along with other artefacts, an Egyptian mummy was on display.

'I will come and see that mummy the next time I am in this city,' he told himself before dialling Ashfaq's number. 'I'll bring the kids too.'

Five minutes later, he got a call from an unknown number. The man spoke Hindi with a heavy accent. He asked him to walk towards Esplanade and take the first right on Sudder Street and wait for him in front of the red church. 'A 10-year-old boy will come to you with a black plastic bag and you will put the package in it. Then you will wait right there while I check the good and send the money,' he said.

Lakhan did not have much trouble finding the church. An urchin approached him with a black bag as the man had said. The boy in black shorts and a shabby grey T-shirt came right up to him, held out the bag and said, '*Isme daal do.*' *Put it in here.*

So he did and the boy turned and left.

After a short while, he saw the boy again. He was still carrying the black bag but the contents seemed to have changed. The call came just as he handed the bag over to Lakhan.

'You will find the agreed-upon cash in the bag. It's in non-sequential 1,000-rupee notes,' said the man from the other end of the phone.

Lakhan took a deep breath. His work was done. Ashfaq

had said this was an old client and he did not need to count the money to check if everything was all right.

He wanted to fly back, especially because of the long and tiring journey he made by road. But that would be risky considering the amount of black money he had on his person. He booked an AC First Class berth on the Rajdhani Express that evening.

By Sunday evening, Harold and Patel had been tailing Dr Sankar Ghosh for nearly two days and had considerably more information than they did on Friday night—most of it from Sankar talking on the phone from home.

2012

BORN TO BE A LAWYER

Narendranath Mukherjee was born on 15 September 1947, a month after India achieved Independence from British rule, into a family of lawyers. He was the only son to have been born to his father Debendranath Mukherjee. One of the first things he learnt about the profession was attorney–client privilege.

'When you become a lawyer, *Dadubhai*,' his grandfather Chandranath used to say, 'you can never reveal to anyone else what your client tells you. It is not only a legal bond, but also one of trust.' Chandranath never for a moment could imagine that his grandson would grow up to be anything but a lawyer.

'Yes, *Dadu*,' was the stock reply of the teenage Narendranath, whom everybody called Naru. It was not that he could not imagine himself becoming a lawyer, but just a fact that he had secretly been considering several other options. Of course, he could never reveal what was on his mind to his family, especially his grandfather.

Chandranath was a highly respected lawyer in the Calcutta High Court and he continued to work until a week before his passing away in 1965. The 80-year-old lawyer had been making the closing statement of a case—he was confident of a favourable verdict—when he collapsed. Debendranath, who was at the high court canteen at that moment, was immediately informed. With the help of several colleagues, he rushed his father to Calcutta Medical College.

The old man returned home three days later once he had recovered from the heart attack. Their family doctor and old friend, Samir Kumar Ghosh, came to see him the same evening.

'Dada, you are elderly. It is time you took it easy and passed on your responsibilities to the next generation,' said the doctor.

'You are right, Samir. That realisation dawned on me only after I came to my senses at the hospital,' said Chandranath, his baritone, which had made many a lawyer on the other end nervous over the years, still intact. He then looked Samir in the eye and said, 'And I have not forgotten my responsibilities.'

Samir nodded quietly.

Later that night after everyone was done with dinner, Chandranath summoned his son and grandson to his room.

'Close the door, *Dadubhai*,' he told his grandson.

The 18-year-old did that and returned to sit beside his father in front of his grandfather's bed, where the old man lay. Chandranath looked tired.

'*Dadubhai*, I do not need to remind your father about what I am going to ask you now, because he is a professional, and from what I hear, quite good at his job.' He smiled and so did his next two generations. 'But to you, I will ask if you remember all that I have told you about attorney–client privilege.'

'Yes, *Dadu*, I do.'

'Explain it to me.'

'A lawyer must not divulge to a third party all that his client has revealed to him,' he said.

Chandranath smiled. 'I couldn't have said it better myself. Do you know what a will is?'

'It is what you want to be done with your property once you are dead.'

'Quite right,' said the old man. 'I am not going to live much longer, *Dadubhai*, and I have already handed over my will to your father.'

The teenager kept quiet and stared at the floor.

'But it is okay. Everyone gets there. Even you will, one day. The point is to live a worthwhile life, and I believe I have been able to do that,' Chandranath said. 'But the reason I have called the two of you here today is because law is not the be-all and end-all in all spheres of our lives. You are my lawyers today and I, your client. It is of utmost importance that you do not reveal to a third party anything that I am about to tell you now, at least not before the time is right.'

'But I am not a lawyer,' protested the teenager.

'You will be soon enough,' said the old man. 'And this will be good practice.'

'What do you mean?' Debendranath spoke for the first time.

'In my will, son, I have bequeathed to you something that is legally mine, but not actually. I am just a guardian, as I hope you will be when I am no more,' said his father, looking at both his son and grandson as he spoke the last bit.

By the time the somewhat dazed father and son came out of Chandranath's room shortly before midnight, Narendranath Mukherjee had already decided that he wanted to be nothing but a lawyer.

Four days later, Chandranath Mukherjee had another heart attack. This time, he did not survive it.

A couple of days after he had passed away, Samir came to visit and offer his condolences to the family. He sat in the living room with Debendranath and the latter's wife, Supriya.

When Supriya excused herself and left the room, Debendranath caught the doctor's eye, lowered his voice and said, 'Don't worry, your secret is safe with our family.'

Both of them then turned in the same direction to look at something.

'I cannot thank you enough,' Samir said. He clasped Debendranath's hands before he left.

2012

THE TEXT MESSAGE

The Gellars landed in Kolkata on Sunday evening and a hotel car picked them up.

This was not Ronald's first visit to the city. He had come here twice while researching for his DPhil thesis on British architecture in Victorian Kolkata. During his time as a teacher, he had also been invited by a few universities in Kolkata on several occasions.

But the last time he was here was more than a decade and a half ago and things had changed.

The airport certainly had. Kolkata did not handle as many major international flights as it used to in the early days. But a swanky new terminal was coming up right next to the old one.

Another major change was that of the government. The state had been ruled by a Left Front government for more than three decades since 1977. But now, they looked all but wiped out. From hundreds of billboards across the city, only one face smiled at you—that of the current firebrand chief minister Mamata Banerjee, who, he had heard, wanted to transform Kolkata into London. 'I wonder why,' Ronald murmured to himself.

He was a little disappointed for not being able to stay at his favourite hotel this time. During his last two visits to the city, he had stayed at the Great Eastern hotel.

Confectioner David Wilson had started the hotel way back in 1840. Since then, the hotel grew from strength to strength and had become popular as the Jewel of the East and India's most famous hotel at one point. It played host to many famous personalities including Mark Twain and Queen Elizabeth II. The Great Eastern Hotel had closed down in 2005. A new management had taken over and was renovating it at the moment. It would only be opened the following year.

But the Grand Hotel, now known as The Oberoi Grand, where they were staying this time, was no less steeped in history.

They reached the hotel, situated bang in the centre of the city, around 8 pm. The first call Ronald made once he reached the hotel was to Sankar.

'This is Ronald Gellar. Just to let you know that I am in Kolkata.'

'Welcome! Do you want to meet this evening? Or are you tired? Would you prefer to do it tomorrow?'

'I am a little tired from the journey but I really wouldn't like to keep this waiting. Would you mind coming over to my hotel for a chat in some time?'

'Sure, I can do that. Is it okay if I reach in an hour or so?' said the doctor as he looked out of his window and frowned.

'That should be perfect,' said Ronald.

Sankar disconnected the call and dialled Eva's new Kolkata number. 'Are you busy?'

'Not really. Just having dinner. Are they here?' Eva screamed over the live music that was on at the pub. 'Could you text me please? I can hardly hear anything here.'

Sankar texted Eva that he had the feeling he was being followed. There was a white sedan he could see from the window of his drawing room parked some way away from his house. Though he was not a hundred per cent sure, he was fairly certain he had seen the same car in his rear-view mirror a number of times over the past day or two.

The text, instead of the call, made all the difference, because Patel couldn't pick up that bit of information.

The doctor reached Ronald's hotel and called him. They decided to meet at the hotel's famed Chowringhee Bar.

Ronald and Nathan—both appeared to have just showered—came down in a few minutes. Once the pleasantries were done, Ronald said, 'I'll get right to the point. Do you happen to know someone called Chandu*da*?' He pronounced the name slowly, making every effort to do it correctly.

'It doesn't strike one right away, but that is a common enough name from around here. Let me think,' said Sankar.

'I am sure I do not need to remind you. But try to think from your grandfather's perspective,' said the professor.

'Give me a minute.' Sankar closed his eyes and tried to recall that name.

'I have a little bit of more information. See if it helps. Samir apparently visited his house really often for chat sessions with Chandu*da* in the evenings.'

Like a sudden flash of light, it came to Sankar. 'I know who you are talking about. Is it in his house?'

'At some point, it used to hang in their drawing room. But no one could see the painting in question, of course. I just hope it's still there.'

'Me too,' said Sankar. 'Please excuse me while I make a call.'

Sankar called somewhere to find out a phone number and when he did, he called up the person and spoke to him in Bengali for a short while. Once he disconnected the call, he looked at Ronald and Nathan and said, 'Let's go.'

The three of them got into Samir's car and the doctor asked his driver to take them to Sovabazar.

A white sedan followed Samir's grey Audi SUV. A blue hatchback followed the white sedan.

Since it was a Sunday night, the roads were fairly empty. They drove up Central Avenue and reached Jagat Mukherjee Park at Rajballavpara. From there, they took a left and stopped in front of a narrow by-lane.

'This should be it,' said the doctor and climbed out of the car. Ronald and Nathan followed.

The three of them walked into the by-lane with Sankar squinting his eyes to identify the numbers of the old houses in the dim glow of the nearest street light. He stopped by one and tried to find a bell to ring. He couldn't. So, he rattled the latch on the door a couple of times.

'*Ek minute*,' a male voice hollered from somewhere inside. *One minute*. A few moments later, a shadow appeared on a first-floor balcony. '*Kay?*' *Who is it?*

'Is it Naru*da*? This is Sankar,' the doctor said in Bengali.

'Oh, yes. Just wait. I will be down in a moment.'

They heard steps descending down a staircase and then the door opened. It was rather dark inside and difficult to have a clear view of the person who opened the door. 'I am sorry, the light here stopped working yesterday. I need to get it changed.'

'That's okay,' smiled Sankar. 'May we come in?'

'Please do. It has been a long time since you've visited.'

'That is true. It's been almost 50 years.'

The stranger guided them up the stairs, which opened on the left corner of a balcony running along the side of the building on the first floor. There was a line of rooms behind the balcony. He took them to the first room on the right.

'How old is this house?' asked Ronald as they entered the room.

'Around 85 years,' said the stranger.

They entered a large drawing room through an arched door that had colourful glasses on the curved portion above. The room looked straight out of period film set a hundred years ago.

The door to the room was on its left and once you entered, there were four big old-fashioned sofas facing each other with a big oval table in the space between them. You could imagine this was a place dedicated to meeting up with people and chatting—*adda*, as the Bengalis call it—because there was not even a television set in the room. On the wall facing the door was a clock and two not-very-big paintings. One of them was of a boat in the Ganga and the other of a clay artist creating an idol of Goddess Durga.

Both the Gellars fixed their stares on these two, because they seemed more or less the right size.

They sat with their backs to a bookshelf, Sankar on the left sofa and the stranger on the one on their right.

'I'm Narendranath Mukherjee. And no, it's not in those,' said the man, who had caught the British gentlemen staring at the two smaller paintings in the room. Both of them smiled sheepishly.

'Ronald and Nathan, meet Naru*da*. He is a busy lawyer,' said Sankar.

Narendranath nodded and smiled, 'Not that busy, and please just call me Naru. It's less complicated and I prefer it.'

Naru was about five years older to Sankar. He was short, bald and had a pot belly.

'And Naru*da*, this is Ronald and his son, Nathan. They both arrived from the UK earlier today,' said Sankar.

'Could I interest you in some whisky? Or maybe a beer?'

'A beer would be nice, thank you,' said Ronald. Nathan nodded as well.

'Just a glass of cold water for me, please,' said Sankar.

Three minutes later, the Gellars and Naru sat with a mug of beer in each of their hands, and Sankar was sipping chilled water from his glass.

Naru started talking. 'So, from what I understand, all of you are here looking for a particular painting.'

'Before we go into that, I have a question for Sankar,' said Nathan. 'What's about this *da* thing? Why do you call him Naru*da* when his name is actually Naru? I just realised it's also Chandu*da*. Is the name actually Chandu?'

Both Sankar and Naru burst into laughter.

'*Da* is short for *dada*, meaning elder brother. That's the common way to address people who are a little older to you around here,' explained Naru.

'Our house used to be in the next lane and we would often hang out and play together as kids,' said Sankar. 'But it was such a long time ago. Our families were close too. My grandfather would come over in the evenings to chat with his friends right here in this room. Chandu*da* is Naru*da*'s grandfather. His real name was Chandranath Mukherjee, but most people close to him called him Chandu.'

'And yes, Samir and Bates indeed left something in the possession of my grandfather,' said Naru.

'Where is it?' asked Ronald.

'In this very room. But not where you were looking,' he grinned. 'It's that one,' he said and pointed at the biggest painting in the room—the one of the 1940s Esplanade.

Everyone in the room turned to look at the painting.

'I can't believe it,' said Ronald under his breath. 'After all these years…'

'You will find that the painting has an unusually heavy frame and that the back is solid wood. It's supposed to be inside, but then, I have never opened it to check myself. That is just what I have been told. But now that Sankar is here with the two of you, I think we can go ahead and open it right now if you wish,' said Naru.

'However much I would like to do that,' said Ronald, 'I think it would be extremely unfair to not share that moment with all the other people who have had a part to play in the discovery of this painting.'

'If you say so,' said Naru. 'I should tell you my duty in this matter ends here, because all I was supposed to do was hand this over to someone from the family of Samir Kumar Ghosh when they came to ask for it, and now you have.' He said the last bit looking at Sankar.

'Your contribution is no less than anyone else's, possibly more than everyone else's since it was with you this entire time. I would really like it, and I am sure Ronald would too, if you come over to the Grand Hotel tomorrow morning with the painting when everyone is present and open it right there,' said Sankar.

'I think that's an excellent idea,' said Ronald and Nathan nodded in agreement.

Naru smiled. 'Thank you. It would be my pleasure.'

The two men did not speak but just stared at the building and the SUV parked nearby from some 50 metres away from them. The blue car was nowhere to be seen. But Neil was right there, appearing busy on the phone but keeping a watch on everything around.

At 11.30 pm, the three men left the old building. The people in the white car looked extra carefully to check if they were carrying anything with them. They weren't.

The SUV headed back to Esplanade. The white sedan stealthily followed it. The blue hatchback followed the white sedan.

'You hang out with my wife when you are working. Now that you're on leave, you want to hang out with me?' said Shreya's husband Prakash into the phone.

'Shut up,' I laughed.

'Why else would you call me at midnight?' he said in a mock-angry tone.

'I think I could do with some help from you tomorrow, Mr Crime Branch.'

'You only call me when you want to get work done. And what's about this German girl with cute dimples? I hear you're never leaving her side these days?'

'I'll tell you all about her and get you to meet her. But first hear me out, because this is really big. I need some protection for a painting from tomorrow for a couple of days,' I said.

'Go ahead,' said Prakash, whom I had known for seven years.

I told him in short the incredible journey of this painting that was thought to be lost and how some people worked so hard so that it survived. He was impressed. I told him we had located the painting but there were already people after it, but that we believed they were just keeping a watch on the proceedings at the moment and were not sure if we had actually located the artwork. However, they would probably figure that out by tomorrow and that was when we needed to be careful. Prakash promised to be there at the Grand Hotel with a couple of men at noon. He also promised to keep the involvement of the crime branch unofficial unless absolutely necessary.

You do not want politicians with vested interests getting involved in such matters.

2012

TIME FOR A CHAT

Mid-morning on Monday, 4 June, Ronald and Nathan Gellar, Sankar and Ivy Ghosh, and Eva Schicktanz sat at La Terrasse, the all-day dining restaurant of the Oberoi Grand.

They exchanged introductions and recounted the events till date. Some time later, they shifted to Ronald's room, deciding it would be more comfortable there. Ronald offered everyone beer, opened one himself, and said, 'I quite enjoy starting my mornings with beer! Now, where were we?'

'They stole my stuff in Magdeburg and were trying to follow us even on the train,' said Eva. 'We managed to lose them on the way though. But they may have caught up with me again when I returned to my place in Berlin.'

'So you told Sankar the phrase after you returned to Berlin, right?' asked Ronald.

'It was quite by accident. I had this phrase and the letter said it was required to be spoken at the right place or to the right person. We weren't sure which it was then. Neil and I thought it could have something to do with the person who made the fake painting or paintings and I called up Sankar to find out about that guy. But when I told Sankar I have this phrase to tell someone, he was like, "Tell me now!"'

Everyone laughed.

'That's about it. Sankar asked me to come over and here I am,' said Eva.

'Now you, Sankar,' Ronald said.

'Well, I heard the detailed story of how Bates came to Kolkata and fell seriously ill from my father and what happened thereafter,' said the doctor. 'Actually, I think my grandfather only told my father the essential bits. My father told me how Bates had been trying to save this painting that the world thought was destroyed. And he said, one day, someone from Germany would come to me and tell me a simple phrase based on the information on the painting that I had. This person would be related to Jonas Bormann and would have read that phrase in a letter.'

Ronald interrupted. 'So you didn't know the phrase?'

'No. That would defeat the purpose of the entire exercise.'

'True. But you did know that the painting was in Kolkata, right?'

'Of course. I just didn't know where. That's where you come in. After I had been told the phrase, I was supposed to call up the head of the History of Art department at Oxford University and say the same words to him or her. That I did, and the information reached you.'

'This is fascinating. Did you know about this, Ivy?' Nathan said.

'I did,' smiled the doctor's wife.

Then Ronald continued, 'I worked under and then with Walter Bates at Oxford. Walter was the elder brother of Edward. The call from Kolkata with the phrase was originally intended for him. Shortly before he was due to retire, he called me one evening in 1971 and told me the entire story. He said all the heads of department knew about this phrase and if Walter wasn't the head when the call came, their job was basically to transfer the call to him. No one else knew what it was about. Walter chose me as kind of his successor so that in his absence I was able to carry out the duty his brother had assigned to him.'

2012

WHAT HAPPENED AT THE RED LIGHT

I borrowed a friend's car—another blue hatchback, but of a different make—just in case the other party had noted my car number before and got suspicious finding me hanging around them.

I drove to Sudder Street at 8 am, found a parking spot close to the hotel and kept watch. I was surprised when they didn't leave before 9.45 am to go to the Grand Hotel. How could they possibly know that Naru was going to leave his home after 11 am (if they were going there, which I was sure they would)? If the possibility of them having planted a listening device somewhere hadn't occurred to me before that, it did right then. I remembered the man who called himself a researcher who had been to Sankar's and had told him the phrase. He could have done that. If Sankar's home was bugged, they sure knew a lot of things at this point.

When the two men came out of the hotel, both the men were in jeans and collared T-shirts. While the white man's shirt was grey, the Indian guy—the apparent researcher—wore a light brown one. Each carried a sling bag. The Indian guy was on the phone as they came out. They waited in front of the hotel for two minutes before a white Swift Dzire taxi—the same car from last night—turned up. They got in and the car zoomed ahead. I followed.

When the car took Central Avenue and went north, I had little doubt in my mind as to where they were heading. The sedan turned left at Rajballavpara and parked at the exact same spot as it had the previous night.

Shortly afterwards, Naru left his house and he was not alone. He had two men carrying a big, flat, rectangular package. Far too big, I thought. And it looked heavy. The three of them walked across the narrow lane off Madan Mohan Tala Street, where his house was, and unlocked a red Suzuki Ritz with an 'Advocate, Calcutta High Court' sticker on its back windscreen. He opened the boot and the two men placed the package there before leaving. Naru then got into the driver's seat and drove out. The sedan followed.

The two men had been 99 per cent sure that the painting was at the house of Naru. They became 100 per cent sure when, on the morning of 4 June, Patel heard Sankar saying to his wife, 'Get ready quick! *Naru pouchhe jaabe dupur barotay!*'

The second sentence was in Bengali, and since it was not too different from Hindi, Patel caught the words '*dupur barotay*', 12 noon, apart from Naru. He quickly wrote them down and went to the reception to have the sentence translated.

'Naru will reach at 12 noon,' said the smiling young receptionist and gladly accepted a 10-rupee note from Patel.

The two men looked at each other. 'There is only one reason that guy is coming to the meeting tomorrow,' said Harold once they were out of earshot of the receptionist.

'It sure seems so. But can we be totally sure of this?'

'If we go by the pass-phrase "From Arles to Calcutta", we have to assume the painting is in this city. All the evidence is anyway pointing to that. And the only other Kolkata connection we see here apart from Sankar is this Naru guy. We know for sure Sankar does not have the painting. The local guy with Eva is just involved in the whole affair by accident. Who's left? Naru. They visit him at midnight right after they arrive. So we know it's urgent or that they cannot wait and it sure has been a long time. Now we know he is coming to the meeting at noon. So, he is definitely crucial here and wants to make an entrance with the prize,' said Harold.

'In that case, we should get him before he reaches there,' said Patel.

'Do you have a plan? It's crowded and in the middle of the day.'

'We will go smooth and no one 10 feet away will realise what just happened. And I think we will also be able to take them by surprise, since they will never expect us to go about it that way.'

They left right on time in the same car they had been using since Patel got to Kolkata. Patel paid 3,000 Indian rupees to the driver every day, and he drove them anywhere they wanted and did not ask questions. Both Patel and Harold preferred working with people who were like that.

The road was crowded, as expected on a Monday morning. They parked at the same spot they were at the previous night because from there, it was possible to have a good view of the entrance to Naru's house.

They had to wait for less than half an hour before Naru emerged with the two men carrying a package.

The two men looked at each other and nodded.

'Park to his left at the next signal,' said Patel to the driver. Both Harold and Patel were sitting in the back seat and were wearing false beards that covered most of their faces. Harold was even wearing sunglasses. The next signal happened to be at the Sovabazar crossing, where the clock on the traffic lights showed there were still some 70 seconds to go; most drivers turned off their ignition. Naru did the same, and that was what they had been waiting for. As soon as Patel, sitting on the right, heard the engine of the red car next to him being switched off and the automatic door locks clicking open, he jumped out, with Harold following.

He calmly opened the door on the left of the driver's seat and sat down on the seat next to Naru. When a shocked Naru turned to protest, he started at the Mauser, pointing at him from under the sling bag that was now placed on Patel's lap.

'Don't speak,' hissed Patel, looking into Naru's eyes. 'And open the boot.'

Harold had already placed himself behind the boot and as soon as it opened and he tried to pick up the package, he realised it was heavier than he had thought it would be. But it was not unmanageable. He pulled it out, said a cheerful and loud 'thank you', placed it on the road for two seconds as he closed the boot, and lifted it behind his own car, the boot of which was already open. His driver ran up to help him and they both lifted the package into the boot and slammed it shut. Then both Harold and the driver got into the car, cheerfully smiling at Patel.

In a few moments, the lights turned green and Patel said, 'There are six bullets in this gun. You have absolutely no chance of getting away alive if I start shooting. So drive straight and give me your phone.'

Still shocked, Naru handed over his phone, which Patel promptly switched off and slipped into his pocket. After a bit, Patel asked Naru to take a left while the white sedan moved straight ahead.

If I wasn't mistaken, the Indian guy gave Naru a smile and a wave before opening the door and getting in his car. That completed the illusion of acquaintance. I was sure he had some kind of a weapon—probably a gun—and that's why Naru hadn't raised an alarm.

When the traffic lights turned green and both the cars moved forward, I followed. After a bit, when the red hatchback turned left and the sedan went straight ahead towards Esplanade, I hesitated for a bit, wondering which car to follow—Naru in one and the painting in the other. Ultimately, I decided to go after the white sedan because that's where the painting was and everything that was happening at the moment was about the painting.

At the Mahatma Gandhi Road and Central Avenue intersection when the red lights stopped both the sedan and me, I managed to calm down and called up Prakash, who was about to reach the hotel, and asked him to come directly to Sudder Street.

The light had turned green by the time we had finished talking and I noticed Eva was calling me. I picked up, gave her a quick update, and cut it. I looked ahead to see the cars already moving and panicked when I realised I had lost the sedan.

2012

THE SPY'S BROTHER

Ronald put his beer bottle aside and said, 'Both Edward Bates and Herr Bormann could guess the fact that the person who wanted to acquire the painting—a certain Mr Pemberton—never intended to return it to the Magdeburg gallery once the war ended. Consequently, the two of them chalked out a plan to ensure he never got his hands on the original in the first place.'

The room was silent and all eyes were on Ronald.

He continued, 'The official plan was simple. Get a single copy made of the painting and have it replaced with the original. Then, Bates was to take the original back with him to England and hand it over to the guy. However, since the mission concerned an artwork, and he didn't know much about art, he decided to discuss it with his brother, Walter. And that discussion changed everything.

'Walter told Edward that he could not believe his brother was going to help steal a piece of art created by one of the world's greatest artists. Edward tried to convince him that it was not stealing and that he was actually helping save it. If they left it to its fate, it was most certainly going to be destroyed or stolen anyway.

'But Walter was not convinced. He told him that just because someone could steal it later did not mean it was right for him to be party to stealing it first. Edward said it was a government mission and he could do nothing about it. Walter told him that since Edward would be working alone in Magdeburg armed with a letter from the prime minister himself, he could, in fact, make a substantial bit of difference if he really wanted. The two brothers had a big argument that night and evidently, Edward slept on it because the next morning, he came to Walter and asked him what he could do about the entire situation.

'They chalked out an elaborate plan, of which, apart from me, the two of you,' Ronald said looking at Eva and Sankar, 'became a part of.'

Eva interrupted, 'So how was it supposed to work? It seems to me no one knew the entire plan.'

Ronald smiled. 'That was the beauty of it. Everyone was only supposed to do their bit. That way, no one would know the location of the painting, and even if a part of the plan was compromised, the bad guys could go only till a certain point and no further. But the thing is, what they worked out was only a theory of how Edward could go about it because he still hadn't been to Germany and didn't know who were going to be part of it.'

'But how did he know Herr Bormann would be party to the plan?' I asked.

'He didn't. So when he first met him as a potential partner, all he told him was that he was working for the British government and that his government wanted to save that painting from getting destroyed.'

'Did Herr Bormann buy it?' I asked.

'Not at all. He asked him to cut the crap because he believed this was just an excuse for the British to steal the painting,' said Ronald.

'I believe that's when Bates told him his true intentions?'

'Yes. They realised things would be simpler if they both survived the war. But they also made elaborate plans in case they didn't. First, they got two copies made instead of one. Then Herr Bormann wrote a letter with the phrase, which he had decided with Bates the night before they left for Stassfurt, because Bates had got to know only a couple of days earlier that he would be going to Kolkata shortly afterwards, and he intended to carry the painting with him. He kept it at a place where Claudia was sure to find it.

'It took Herr Bormann more time than he had anticipated to extract the original from the frame. He didn't even find enough time to properly fix the fake in the original's frame because of the fire. Bates had a narrow escape and Herr Bormann couldn't make it outside the mine alive. As much as Bates wanted, he decided not to visit Claudia but escaped with the painting to London at the earliest. He sent the message of Herr Bormann's death through the British army to Claudia.

'Back in England, he handed over the second fake painting to the office and then spent a couple of days at home before heading out to India. During this time, he discussed his plan further with Walter and told him that he had already set it in motion.'

'But why didn't he just hide it somewhere in the UK?' Nathan said.

'That's because Bates anticipated that sooner or later, they would find out that the painting they had was a fake, and if it was still in the UK, it would have been easier for them to find out. Before leaving, Edward told Walter the key phrase and that is all he knew at that point.'

'Then how'd you know about Chandu*da*?' said Ivy.

'I'll come to that,' said Ronald. 'Like Sankar knows, a British officer came to see Bates a number of times when he was on his deathbed. What he didn't know was that he was an ally. He was an old friend of Bates and agreed to help. Samir knew about him of course. But what you have known till now is the story he was supposed to tell you. It was all part of the plan.'

'What was it that actually happened?' Sankar asked.

'After he arrived in India, Bates had actually kept the painting with that officer, whose name, I am afraid, I do not know. It was he who arranged to get the messages sent to Claudia and Walter—to Claudia with the information on the doctor, and to Walter with the name of Chandu*da*.' Ronald smiled again. 'However, this British officer did not know where the painting was hidden in Kolkata. That information was privy to only Bates and Samir.

'Samir, we now know, hid it in a different painting and gave it as a present to Chandu*da*, who, of course, knew his present was more than just the painting that everyone could see. He told everyone else the new painting in the room was a present from Samir and under no circumstances was it to be removed from there. He passed on the actual information to his eldest son and to his grandson Naru.

'So, how it was supposed to happen was, after the war got over, Claudia was expected to connect two and two—the pass-phrase in Herr Bormann's letter and reference to the doctor in Bates' letter. Both Herr Bormann and Bates expected her to make the connection because she knew about the painting. But they also considered the possibility of her not figuring it out, or choosing not to pursue it. So, the plan was supposed to be a long-lasting one, which it was, as you see. If Claudia had been able to get in touch with Samir when he was alive, he could have given the painting to her, so that she could return it to the museum. But if things didn't work that way, they were prepared to handle it. The idea was that, however late it was, the painting should return to the museum.'

'And so it shall,' said Eva, giving him a thumbs up.

'Sankar, where is our man of the moment, Naru?'

'He is supposed to be here by 11.30 latest, but I'll just check,' he said and dialled the number on his mobile phone. After a moment of silence, his brows knitted in worry. 'His phone is switched off. Eva, could you try calling Neil?'

Eva dialled Neil's number and he picked up. 'I'm driving, can't talk. Naru's been kidnapped and the package is with the other party. I'm after them. I'll call in a bit,' he said and disconnected.

Eva told everyone what she just heard. Everyone sat stunned in pin-drop silence, waiting for the phone to ring.

I drove as fast as I could, looking left and right on the road like crazy until I reached Sudder Street to find Prakash parking his car. I called out to him, parked behind him and ran up the steps to the hotel.

Prakash flashed his ID and asked about the two men who had left in a white cab earlier in the morning. 'What rooms are they in?' he asked.

'Sir, they were in 205 and 206,' said the receptionist.

'Were? Did you say "were"? Aren't they still here? They have not checked out!' I said.

'Yes, sir, they did this morning,' he said.

I couldn't believe it. 'What are you saying? I saw them leave with just two sling bags. Surely, they had more luggage?' I asked.

'They did. But they had packed early and already kept the bags in their car, and checked out. They had breakfast in their room and stayed in 206 till close to 10. Then they left in the car.'

'I would like to see their entry in the booking records,' said Prakash.

The receptionist showed them the records of a Donald Yardley from London and a Rakesh Singh from Gurgaon. Prakash pointed at the pictures and looked at me.

'I have mostly seen them inside cars, but these sure look like them. But I don't know their names,' I said.

'Probably fake IDs,' said Prakash, and we left the hotel. He sat in my car and made five quick calls. Then he said, 'Now that they have the painting, they will try leaving the country as soon as possible. I have the railway stations covered as best I can unofficially, using my contacts. I am also trying to check out CCTV feeds on roads leading out of the city. I cannot promise you anything, Neil. But I sure am trying my best. I guess you should go to the hotel and update the others on the situation.'

2012

THE WHITE SEDAN

When an agitated Neil was talking on the phone, the white sedan took a left from Mahatma Gandhi Road and went straight ahead until it reached Sealdah Railway Station. Harold's destination was VIP road, because that was where he was supposed to pick up Patel.

If Neil had not been convinced that the sedan was headed to Sudder Street, he would probably have looked left while crossing Mahatma Gandhi Road and seen the car moving slowly behind a battered blue bus. Instead, he was frantically searching for it in the sea of cars in front of him.

The white car went straight to Khanna crossing, turned right and headed towards Ultadanga. Once there, it took the VIP road towards the airport. It slowed down and stopped by the road near Lake Town. Shortly afterwards, another cab slowed down and stopped behind it. Patel got out of that one, walked ahead and slipped into the seat beside Harold in the back.

'No problem?' Harold asked.

'No problem,' Patel answered.

The car rolled into the road, crossed the airport entrance, and took the Beleghata bypass. After 40 minutes, it had crossed the toll gate on National Highway 2 and was racing at 110 kmph towards Burdwan. It was one in the afternoon and they would take close to seven hours to reach their destination, which lay far beyond Burdwan.

In the evening, Prakash found the six of them at Chowringhee Bar, the hotel's pub, sitting at the table with beers. No one was talking. He took a beer himself and joined them at the table. I introduced him to the gang.

'We have found Mr Mukherjee. He was sitting in his car by Basanti Highway, drugged. They probably used a syringe, but we haven't been able to find that yet. But the good news is he should be perfectly normal soon,' said Prakash. 'Oh, come on! All is not lost. Why are all of you so morose?'

'With due respect, sir, I think you are failing to understand the historical significance of the situation,' said Nathan.

'Probably. I'm not so much into arty stuff. But I know that sitting here and moping will make nothing better,' said the policeman.

'Agreed. What do you suggest we do?'

'Watch a movie! I could recommend a Bengali potboiler that's running now. It will have you in splits even if you don't understand a word anyone is saying,' smiled Prakash.

'I think that's the one Neil and I went for the other day,' grinned Eva.

‘See, even the thought of the film makes you happy,’ said Prakash. ‘I should have some news for you by tomorrow morning. I’ll pass on the message through Neil.’

Sankar and Ivy decided to go home while Eva and I decided to go over to my place. I assured Ronald, who looked 10 years older than he looked that morning, that I would up keep him updated with developments.

As we drove home, Eva went quiet. I turned to her to see her with her jaw clenched. I held her hand.

‘We were so close. I couldn’t even see it with my own eyes,’ she said.

‘We will,’ I assured her. ‘They will never be able to take it out of the country.’

‘Can you promise me that?’

I smiled. ‘Prakash has promised me just that, and he tends to keep his promises.’

It was evening when the white sedan reached Dhanbad station. While the two men, who still had their beards on, walked to the station with their sling bags and travel suitcases, the driver carried the heavy flat package.

You do not get your seat numbers when you book AC First on Indian Railways, because seats are limited and the railway people just accommodate people according to their discretion. The passengers get to know their seat numbers once the passenger list for the train is prepared a couple of hours prior to departure. Patel looked up the reservation list at the railway station and quickly identified their compartment.

When every other train is running late in India, the trains that are most likely to be running close to schedule are the Rajdhani Expresses, which run from various parts of the country to the *rajdhani*, meaning capital, which in the case of India is New Delhi. This time, too, the train chugged into Dhanbad station at 8 pm—four minutes late. But no one cares about four minutes when it comes to Indian Railways.

The three of them got into their compartment and both Patel and Harold were happy to find they had been allotted a two-person coupé. Patel shook hands with the driver as he got down and stuffed a bunch of currency notes into his hand.

The ticket checker knocked and checked their tickets after the train left the station and the attendant took their orders for dinner. Harold and Patel had lost their beards by then. Both of them sat and chalked out their future plan of action. Patel liked simple and efficient ideas and, especially after how things had gone earlier in the day, Harold had enough faith in his plans.

Patel's idea to take the painting out of the country was simple, too. He wanted to get the painting off the frame, slide it in a secret flat pocket of his check-in bag, which would be subject to less scrutiny, and glide through security. 'It will just be another layer of cloth on the bag's lining. No one will notice it, especially if they are not specifically looking for something,' he said.

This was the first time Harold was travelling on a train in India and he was surprised by how comfortable it was and how good the food was. After dinner was done, Harold latched the door shut and placed the package between them on the lower bunk bed. Patel cut the string that held the cover and removed the brown paper. Old Kolkata smiled at them.

'This is a nice picture,' said Harold. 'It's probably a local artist.'

He took the painting over from Patel and turned it around. It had a solid wood frame. 'Now why would a framed painting have a wooden back?' he said, and took out a small toolkit from his sling bag. From the kit, he brought out a small hammer and chisel and set to work along the side of the frame. He asked Patel to hold the painting vertically on the floor and kept tapping it with the hammer with the chisel placed on the faint joint line visible on the frame. He did it carefully and patiently. You could see he knew what he was doing. He continued the work all along the frame till the faint line became more and more prominent. Then he used the chisel as a lever to separate the front and back of the frame. The process was slow, but Harold was too excited to even get tired. At the end of more than an hour of work, he carefully lifted the back of the painting's frame and kept it aside. Then he turned to see a painting sitting snug in a frame specially built to fit into the back of the bigger one.

It was just as he had imagined it. After 70 years in the dark and without care, it sure looked a wee bit dull—but not something an expert hand couldn't fix. The first place his eyes went to was the row of five leaves. Yes, the third and fourth were significantly smaller than the rest. He nodded silently. A smile had touched his lips even though Harold wasn't even aware of it. He was in a daze of emotions he couldn't identify and he didn't even care. His quest was complete.

'It's beautiful,' he whispered. It was only then that he realised his eyes were welling up. He had expected he would be ecstatic when he finally got his hands on the masterpiece, but his own emotions surprised him and took him off guard. 'Why the hell am I crying?' he said to himself, rubbing his eyes with the back of his sleeve.

'You have been through a lot to get to it,' said Patel.

Harold did not reply. He just continued to stare at the self-portrait of Vincent van Gogh walking with a roll of canvas in a Mediterranean summer setting.

2012

THE BLUE BAG

It was just past five in the morning when the phone rang. Prakash's voice boomed from the other side when I finally picked it up.

'Get up, sleepyhead! We've located them.'

'Uh...wha...where?'

'Get dressed and pack for a couple of days. We are flying to Delhi in less than two hours. Get your ass to the airport ASAP!'

'Eva's coming too,' I said.

'Yes, yes, I'm getting her ticket. I'll call back in 20 minutes and you should be locking your door and ready to leave by then,' said the cop and disconnected the call.

Eva and I got ready superfast and packed only the stuff that we could carry into the cabin. When we were outside waiting for our cab to arrive, Prakash emailed me our tickets. I did a web check-in on the way to the airport. When we reached we faced a huge queue at security. This was among the busiest times at the airport. We looked at the time frequently and finally cleared security at 6.45 am. We ran to our gate to find the last of the passengers going out of the door but Prakash was sitting on a chair right there.

'There you are. I thought you were going to miss this one,' he said. 'Let's go! We have a busy day ahead.'

Prakash sat in the middle seat while I took the aisle and Eva the window, so that both of us could hear what he had to say.

'These guys knew we would be keeping a watch on the railway stations in the city. So they chose to take a train not from Kolkata but after driving some way ahead,' he said.

'My sources first alerted me after the car passed through a toll gate near Dankuni. From then on, we could track it as it passed through several other toll gates on National Highway 2. The car dropped them at Dhanbad and returned to Kolkata later that night. We caught hold of the driver shortly after he entered the city around two this morning and he said he had dropped the two men at Dhanbad station from where they had taken the Rajdhani Express bound to Delhi. This driver had been acting as their personal chauffeur for the past four or five days. He said the white guy had arrived in Kolkata on 1 June evening.'

Eva interrupted. 'I arrived on 1 June in the evening. Does that mean he was on my flight?'

When Prakash told her Harold's flight number, Eva confirmed it was the same flight as hers. 'The bastard has been following me since then!' she said, horrified.

'So it appears. But we've got both of their actual names because they did not use forged documents to enter the country. The white guy is called Harold Pemberton and the brown guy Ratnesh Patel,' said Prakash.

'Pemberton...why does that name sound familiar?' Eva mumbled to herself. And then she remembered. 'Richard Pemberton was the person who had originally wanted the painting! He was the one who was close to Churchill and had made him commission the mission to save the painting in the first place.'

'Are you sure?' I said. 'How do you know this?'

'You were following those two around the city when Ronald was telling us his side of the story. That's when he told us this.'

'Well, that makes sense,' said Prakash. 'So, let me tell you how we're going to go about things today. We land in Delhi in the morning and take the airport express to New Delhi railway station, where the Rajdhani Express is scheduled to arrive. Even if we are a little late, it doesn't matter because I already have requested a friend of mine to be there. What we're going to do is follow them to wherever they are going and strike at an opportune moment.'

The breakfast on the train was as good as the dinner the previous night. Harold was in a good mood because things were going smoothly. They had gotten both the paintings off their frames the night before. Late at night when everyone was asleep, Patel had thrown the wooden frames off the train. Harold had wanted to get rid of the Esplanade painting as well, but Patel had decided to keep it as a memento.

Once the Van Gogh was off its frame, Harold set his navy blue travel bag on the floor, zipped the cover flap open. The cover flap of the expensive bag was made of thick and tough material. The inside had a see-through compartment where Harold kept his toiletries pouch and other knick-knacks. What was not apparent was the entire see-thorough compartment was attached to the back of the cover with strong Velcro, which Harold, slowly, bit by bit, pulled open. He placed the painting inside two pieces of thin but firm cardboard, clipped the sides so that it did not slide out, and placed it inside the Velcro compartment of the cover. Then he carefully closed it up. You wouldn't know it was there even despite looking closely at the inside of the cover.

They had their plan clearly laid out. They were taking the direct British Airways flight to London early the next morning. Patel had got a contact to pick them up from the train station and take them to a hotel not far away because they intended to take the airport express train that started from there.

When they reached New Delhi, the two men got down with two bags each and headed to the foot overbridge, where a middle-aged man with a thick black moustache and salt-and-pepper hair greeted Patel. They shook hands and he offered to take Harold's big bag, which Harold politely refused. Together, they headed towards Pahargunj.

A man standing on the foot overbridge clicked a picture of the three on his phone as they climbed up, and sent it to someone. 'The two guys walking behind are your men, right?'

'Yes. Thanks for doing this, man. We're reaching in 15,' came the reply from Prakash, who, along with Neil and

Eva, was on the Airport Express heading to the New Delhi railway station.

The train reached their destination and the three ran to Paharganj. Prakash was on the phone all this time talking to his contact. The three waited there for a few minutes, during which at least 10 rickshaw pullers approached them to ask where they would like to go. Then a clean-shaven man in a white shirt, jeans and black glasses approached and hugged Prakash, who introduced him to Neil and Eva as his old friend Arif Khan. He carried a grey sling bag.

Arif walked them through the crowded street, took a left after a bit and pointed at a nondescript two-storey guest house.

'Does he work with the police in Delhi?' whispered Eva to me.

Arif heard her and turned to her with a smile. 'Something like that. I work for the government. Your guys are in there and they have some amount of backup in the form of local contacts. But I cannot be sure how many. Could be just the one guy I saw or could be several more,' he said.

'Do we need backup? Do you have a gun?' Prakash said.

'Yes, I have my gun, but I think three or four guys should be good,' said Arif. 'Hold on.' He made two calls on his phone while we waited. Prakash bought us tea from a street-side vendor and explained to Arif the background of the case.

At length, three tough-looking men with sling bags arrived on a couple of motorcycles. Arif shook hands with them and introduced them to Prakash. They spoke in low tones for a few minutes before Prakash said, 'Neil, I think you should wait here with Eva. There could be some shooting. It wouldn't be safe.'

'Are you kidding me? I've come all the way from Germany for this and you want to keep me out of the action?' said Eva.

'It is not safe, Eva,' Prakash insisted.

Eva had been upbeat since I woke her up at five that morning because she couldn't wait to lay her eyes on the painting that they had lost despite being so close the day before. She took no time to get ready and booked the cab to the airport herself. Her excitement had doubled when she found out Prakash's friend had spotted Harold and Patel in New Delhi. So it was no surprise when she told Prakash that she would like to go to the guest house despite the threat.

'We will be careful,' I promised to Prakash as I realised Eva would not stay back in any case.

Prakash shrugged. 'Stay well behind us and keep your eyes and ears open. And don't get shot.'

The four men went ahead to the guest house. It was a place typical to the area and reminded me of the seedy hotel ironically called Hotel Decent in the Bollywood movie *Jab We Met*.

Arif, who was leading the team, went up straight to the reception, showed the guy there his ID, and said something. The man showed him a huge book—evidently the guest register of the establishment—and Arif nodded.

There was no one else at the reception at the moment.

He said something to the others behind him, who got out their guns from their sling bags. Arif got two out from his and handed over one to Prakash. While one of the men stayed behind at the reception, the others walked stealthily towards the staircase.

The staircase opened in the middle of the first floor and there were two rooms each on both sides. The four men turned left and were out of our sight. We quickly caught up to see Arif snatching away a gun from a man with salt-and-pepper hair and thick black moustache while one of the other cops landed a blow on the moustached man's neck. He moaned.

'All okay, Salman?' came Patel's voice from behind the door.

'Ask him to come out,' hissed Arif into Salman's ear.

'Just come out once, man,' he sounded desperate.

'What's happened?' Patel grew curious.

'Scorpion stung me. Just come out!'

'You're kidding me! There are no scorpions here,' said Patel as he opened the door.

He had fallen for it but he did have the Mauser in his hand. He realised his mistake in a second when he saw three guns pointing at him and a fourth at Salman.

Before he could raise his arm to fire, a shot rang out and he dropped his gun before sitting down and grabbing his right wrist. In no time, people from the other rooms had sheepishly opened their doors to check what had happened, but the cops shooed them back inside. Arif, Prakash and an anonymous guy rushed inside the room screaming 'hands up', pulling along Patel with them, while the other stood guard with Salman outside. We walked gingerly towards the door.

'They don't have any more guns. You can go in,' said one of the guys outside to Eva and me.

Harold appeared to be sitting on the bed with his laptop having a Skype conversation with someone when we barged in. He was just standing up as ordered by Prakash and the rest of them. He looked at us, dumbstruck. He slowly raised his hands over his head. In one of them he held a rolled up handkerchief.

'What's happening, Harold?' said the voice of an old man from the laptop on the bed.

'Is that the senior Pemberton? Is that thief still alive?' said Eva.

'Who is that?' said the man on the screen.

'Jonas Bormann was my grandmother's first husband. I suppose you know him,' said Eva.

'Oh, yes. How the years have passed. I never had the pleasure of meeting him, though,' said Richard.

'I think he died happier because he didn't meet you, Richard Pemberton! You are Richard Pemberton, right?'

'Yes, of course. My son…'

'Yes, your son. Your freaking son,' screamed Eva as she turned to Harold. 'Where the hell is the painting?'

Harold had composed himself by then. He smiled at Eva and said, 'Let me show you,' and sat on the bed again.

'Keep standing,' growled Arif. Harold ignored him and calmly unfolded what had till then looked like a handkerchief in his fingers and spread it on the bed.

Eva and I drew our breaths as we realised it was the canvas separated from its frame. But the bright colours of the Mediterranean summer still mesmerised those who looked upon it.

'What have you done to it?' I said, horrified.

‘I have done nothing to it. I was just showing it to my father here. Just completing his unfinished work. This is my present to him,’ said Harold, unnaturally cool at a time when he was surrounded by people with guns and had zero backup from his side.

‘This is not your present to give, you thief,’ said Eva.

‘Is it not, now?’ He looked at Eva. ‘I will make it simple for all of you. If I cannot have it, neither can you.’

‘You think so, don’t you? And exactly how are you going to accomplish this thing with three guns pointed at your head?’ said Prakash.

‘Like this,’ said Harold and pointed to something behind Eva. The gaze of everyone in the room followed his finger.

In the two seconds that took everyone to realise that the junior Pemberton had pulled a cheap one on them and just pointed to a blank wall, a carving knife had appeared in his hands, with its pointed tip directly on the face of the man in the hat. Everyone drew a collective sharp breath, except Patel, the anonymous man and Arif. The last two men obviously did not understand the importance and significance of the act.

‘Do not do that, Harold. People have died trying to save that painting. Do you have any idea how many people spent how much time and energy to ensure that this painting survived,’ Eva pleaded.

‘I know,’ said Harold in an ice-cold voice. ‘And that is why you will not force me to rip it apart and let me and Patel go.’

‘That’s not going to happen,’ Arif said.

‘It is. Watch me,’ he said and turned to the laptop. ‘Father, as you can see, I am trying my best to save this one for you.

But of course my life is more valuable than a painting. So, I hope you will forgive me if I need to make a hole or two in it.'

'However much I'd love to have it without holes, I love you more than any painting, and if that's what you need to do, that's what you shall do,' said the old man. 'I would also have preferred not to get the High Commission in New Delhi involved. But I think the circumstances now demand that I give them a call. You can expect a call from your foreign ministry shortly, gentlemen,' he said.

'Thank you, Father. You know the name of this guest house. Please mention the name when you make the call. See you soon,' he said and ended the call. Then he looked at Patel and said, 'Are you okay, Patel? Can you walk?'

'I guess I can. I need to get the wound checked, though. The bullet may have broken a bone,' said the man.

To the surprise of everyone in the room, Harold got up, gestured to Patel while holding the painting firmly against the blade of the knife. 'Patel, take my bag with your good hand, will you? And let's go.'

Arif held his gun to Harold's forehead and said, 'Do not mess with me. Hand over the painting and go wherever the hell you want.'

'Look here,' Harold said and he pushed the tip of the knife through the canvas.

A loud, simultaneous 'no' escaped from the lips of Eva and Prakash.

'So you see, I am not bluffing. I don't give a crap about this piece of rag if my security is at stake. You will receive a call from your bosses in a few minutes. And if you do not want to start a diplomatic incident, I suggest you quietly leave while I wait for a car to arrive from the British High Commission,' said Harold.

As if on cue, the guy keeping watch outside the door came in and said, 'Boss, there's a call for you at the hotel reception from the foreign minister's office.'

I noticed that, as Arif cursed and left the room, Harold glanced at his navy blue bag. There was something about that look—it told me that bag was important to him. I tried to catch Prakash's gaze and once I did, I pointed with my eyes to the bag. He nodded.

In a few minutes, Arif came up to the room with a stormy face.

'What?' Eva asked.

'The British High Commission guys will be here in 10 minutes and we are expected to hand over these two pieces of crap to them,' he said, glaring at Harold.

'Did they ask for details?' Prakash asked.

'No. The ministry appeared least interested in that. All they want of us was to keep our hands off whatever this is and let these people go with the High Commission guys when they are here,' he said and glared at Harold.

Harold smiled. 'Yes. That would be nice. No one likes a diplomatic incident at a time when the governments of both India and the UK have such good relations. You have already shot at my aide here and you do not want to make things worse, do you? Moreover, this painting has been lost for 70 years now. Why lose sleep over it? Let it stay just the way it was.'

While the attention of everyone in the room was first on Arif and then on Harold, Prakash moved slowly and stealthily and pulled the bag away towards the door. Both the bag and he had disappeared from the room by the time Harold went on with his rant on how it was better for everyone that the painting remained lost.

Arif received a call from his office telling him the car make and number. It was only when Harold tried to get ready to go downstairs to take the car did he notice that his bag was missing.

'Where is my bag?' Harold said coolly.

'What bag?' I asked in the same tone.

'You know what bag I am talking about,' he growled.

An Indian man in a white shirt and dark trousers came into the room at that point. He looked at the Englishman and said, 'Mr Harold Pemberton?'

'That's me. But I am going nowhere till these guys have returned me my bag.'

'Sir, I work for the British High Commission and have been instructed to transport you and a Mr Ratnesh Patel there at the earliest,' the man said.

'I am going nowhere till I have got my bag,' he repeated.

'Sir, I insist you come right now. It would not be very nice if the press got a whiff of this,' he said.

'I don't care about the bloody press. I need to get my bag before I leave,' Harold yelled.

'Mr Pemberton.' It was Patel speaking this time. 'I think we should just go.'

Harold's face was crimson as he climbed down the stairs and got straight into the back seat of the waiting SUV. Patel followed. The smartly dressed young man got in beside the driver.

At that moment, Prakash appeared on top of the stairs with a smile on his face. 'Mr Pemberton,' he called. 'I found this under the bed in your room.'

Harold turned back to see him coming over to the car with the navy blue bag. His face lit up for one instant before he realised something was wrong. He noticed the big grin Prakash's was sporting. He got down, grabbed the bag, hurled it on the seat of the car, stood outside, and pulled open the zip. Then, he pulled out the back of the flap and revealed the Velcro pouch. It was empty.

'You have a secret pouch in your bag. That is way cool,' Prakash couldn't stop himself from laughing. The other cops realised what had happened and a smile spread across their lips.

Harold crumpled the torn bit of canvas that he had been holding against the knife all this while and put it in his pocket. He got into the car and slammed the door shut.

The SUV zoomed away in a cloud of dust.

2012

AT LONG LAST

It was late night when Eva entered Ronald and Nathan's room at the Oberoi Grand in Kolkata, holding the canvas carefully with her hands. She felt like a celebrity because of the reception she got.

Everyone applauded and cheered and Ronald asked for a bottle of champagne. Today was certainly a day to celebrate.

Shreya had come along as well, for she was interested to see the painting after hearing the entire story from me and Prakash. Sankar and Ivy were there, and so was Mr Narendranath Mukherjee, or Naru.

The champagne arrived in a few minutes and the atmosphere in the room was festive. Everyone who had not been to Delhi was eagerly asking about everything that had transpired at the guest house in Paharganj, and we were only too happy to oblige.

Prakash admitted that it hadn't taken him too long to find the hidden chamber because he knew what he was looking for. 'Simple hiding places such as this one work well when the other party is not looking for something. Airport security might not have noticed it. But since I knew what I was looking for, it did not take me more than five minutes to find it,' he smiled.

Eva kept the canvas on the table and everyone gathered around to have a good look at the painting. Not surprisingly, the first place everyone looked at was the line of five leaves above the painter's hat. All of them were satisfied to find that two of them were significantly smaller.

After Eva, Prakash and I had told everyone the details of what had happened in Delhi earlier in the day, Eva asked me, 'When did you first realise that the painting in Harold's hand was not the original one?'

'There was something about the way he looked at the bag that one instance. He was playing it so cool with the painting in his hand. But that one look he gave the bag gave away that it was important to him. And then it also struck me that at the end of the day, both Harold and Richard were lovers of art. When I thought about it right then, it struck me as supremely odd that not only did Harold appear to not care before putting a knife through such a historic and expensive piece of art, but Richard, the man who had invested so much time, effort, and money on acquiring this painting, dismissed it as being nothing on the excuse of his son's security. It just did not add up. That's when I concluded that the thing in Harold's hand was a fake, quite possibly the one that Bates had handed over to Richard in London all those years ago,' I said.

'That's amazing, Sherlock,' said Eva and kissed me.

'Harold had had enough time to explain his plan to his father before we entered the scene,' I added.

'To Neil,' said Ronald and raised his glass of champagne. The others followed suit.

'What do you want to do with the painting now?' asked Prakash.

'Return it to the Magdeburg gallery, of course,' said Eva.

'And how to plan to go about it?' he asked.

'To tell you the truth, Prakash, I haven't really thought about it. Till today, all I had in mind was getting my hands on the painting. Now that we have it, I am really not sure about how to go about it,' she said.

'In that case, I think what you should do is call up the museum, tell them the situation, and ask them to go about the process through diplomatic channels. Let them make the German Consulate General Kolkata aware of what is happening. Once that is done, you hand the painting over to them. That should be the safest and quickest way if you ask me. Work fast and don't let the damn politicians get involved. If that happens, there will be a hundred people giving you reasons why the painting should stay in India.'

'Thank you for all the help, man,' I said.

'You owe me a beer,' the cop winked.

'Just one? I owe you 10,' I laughed.

'Ladies and gentlemen,' said Ronald. 'May I invite you all to accompany me to dinner? It has been an eventful and successful trip. Tonight, let us celebrate.'

EPILOGUE

When I woke up in the morning, Eva was still asleep. I got off the bed quietly so as not to wake her and gently closed the bedroom door. By the time she came out of the bedroom an hour later, I had a steaming bowl of the Bengali *alur torkari* ready and was frying the last of my *luchis* for breakfast.

'What smells so delicious?' she said, smiling and stifling a yawn at the same time. 'Since when have you been up cooking all this breakfast?'

I went up, kissed her cheek, looked into her eyes and said, 'You know I love you, right?'

'Oh my God, Neil! Finally! Finally.' She laughed. 'I thought you'd never ever say it.'

'Freshen up! The tea will be ready in five,' I smiled.

She went to the bathroom and then came back to the kitchen with a toothbrush sticking out of her mouth. She pulled it out and said, 'You never asked me if I loved you.'

'I know.'

'So? Are you going to ask me now?'

'No!'

She shook her head incredulously. 'Why not?'

'Finish doing your teeth first and come to the table. I'll tell you over breakfast,' I said. I was worried about the *luchi* getting cold.

She was at the table in 10 minutes. 'Now tell me,' she said, leaning over the bowl of *alur torkari* and taking in the aroma.

'Well, nothing would make my day better than you telling me you loved me. But I would never ask you. If you love me, I'd like you to tell me whenever you feel like it. No pressure!'

'So…how about right now?'

'Now is a good time,' I laughed out loud.

'I love you, Neil Bose.'

I smiled and leaned over the table. She took my cue and did the same. Our lips met.

The food had turned out tasty and I loved the look on Eva's face as she clumsily dipped a piece of *luchi* into the yellow potato gravy on her plate before putting it in her mouth. I knew she wasn't just being polite when she said she enjoyed it. 'Shall we make the call today?' she asked.

'We'll do it this afternoon. They wouldn't be open right now,' I said.

We spent the next few hours lazing and just happy to be in the company of each other. It seemed to me Eva was especially happy, for now we were 'officially' in love. I guess telling the other person you loved them did make a difference on some level. I'm not sure what level, but it does bring you closer.

But to me, nothing really had changed. Eva was still the same dimpled girl in uncle-glasses I had fallen in love with last December. And I started to think how wonderful it would be to be able to spend many more Decembers in her company. Well, my mind wanted to imagine and picture several specifics about our future together, but I checked myself. All in good time.

I handed over the phone to Eva in the afternoon. We were lying together on the couch watching the hopelessly romantic *Sleepless in Seattle*.

She took the phone from me and pressed the mute button on the television remote. Then she picked up the big green mug from the centre table in front of us and sipped some tea, before dialling a number in Magdeburg and putting the phone on speaker. A woman picked it up.

'Is this the Kulturhistorisches Museum, Magdeburg?' said Eva in German.

'Ja,' said the voice from the other end.

'Could I speak to the curator, please?'

'Whom shall I say is calling?'

'Tell him…' Eva said and smiled at me. 'Just tell him we've found his Van Gogh.'

ACKNOWLEDGEMENTS

This book wouldn't have been a reality without the support of several people to whom I would like to say thank you.

Teesta Guha Sarkar, for pointing me in the right direction every time.

Annika Bischof, for sending me the couch request that started a chain reaction because of which I now have so many friends in Europe.

Dr Tobias von Elsner, the deputy director at Kulturhistorisches Museum, Magdeburg, for sharing with me promptly all the information I needed.

The helpful people at the library and the IT department at Otto von Guericke University, Magdeburg.

My parents, Shrabani Nandy and Saila Kumar Nandy, for letting me be me.

And Swagata Basu, for being my pillar of support.